Playing on the Roof

Playing on the Roof

Jerry Waxman

authorHOUSE®

AuthorHouse™
1663 Liberty Drive
Bloomington, IN 47403
www.authorhouse.com
Phone: 1-800-839-8640

First published by AuthorHouse   09/19/2011

ISBN: 978-1-4634-1438-2 (sc)
ISBN: 978-1-4634-1435-1 (ebk)

Library of Congress Control Number: 2011909144

Printed in the United States of America

Cover credit: The cover showing Jerry as a child was painted by Jimmy Zimmerman, Jerry's brother-in-law. More of his work can be found at jimzimmermanart.com.

Acknowledgements

$\mathcal{T}$ he efforts of Jerry's loving friends made *Playing on the Roof* possible. The following made particular contributions: Ida Egli and her creative writing class in Gualala, California; Greg Hayes; Kathleen Kraemer; and, especially, Naneene Van Gelder.

Dedication

*I*f Jerry were here to dedicate this book, he would dedicate it to his wife, Pam Zimmerman; his son, Keith Waxman; his daughter, Shannon Boaz, who died of leukemia on November 21, 2009; his sister, Laura Ulric; and his grandsons Charlie Waxman, born October 27, 2009, Jackson Boaz and Austin Boaz.

Foreword

*J*erry's close friends have asked me, "What was Jerry like as a little boy?" They've got a reasonable picture of the man who was my brother, but the question they really seem to want answered is, "What about the child?" O.K. Here goes. Here's the Jerry I knew and loved. Sort of a "Jerry Waxman, this is your life." But without the TV cameras. And without the commercials. And, unfortunately, without Jerry.

Life with Jerry was like an episode in "The Twilight Zone," almost always fun, sometimes painful, and always exciting. Even when he was little, you never knew which Jerry you were going to see. By the time I was born, four years after Jerry, you'd have thought our parents would have gotten it. But they never did. They were always surprised, shocked even, by his antics. His relationship with me was even more bizarre. We were the best of friends growing up, even though he spent a good deal of his time devising new and innovative means of torturing me. But he might actually have had a good reason for that: revenge. Jerry always liked to know the answers to all questions, even those questions that were never asked. My birth didn't fit into that neat niche into which he liked to place things. In fact, we began with a misunderstanding. It seems that through someone's confusion—no one is sure whether it was the doctor or my father—Jerry and the rest of the family had been told that I was a boy. Now, Jerry had really wanted a little brother. When it was made clear to him that I was, indeed, a girl, and that his wish for a brother had been thwarted, what else could he have done but to have made it his life's work to try to behave the way every older brother is supposed to behave toward his little sister? And torture me he did. When he wasn't my bosom buddy.

My mom told me a story about Jerry when he was a little boy, about three years old or so. She had put him to bed at his regular time. I can just picture it: Jerry being tucked in wearing his footed pajamas and looking positively angelic. Notice I said, "looking angelic," not "acting angelic." Mom tiptoed out of the room, closed the door and let out a huge sigh of relief as she sank into the sofa, exhausted after a full day of chasing the ball of energy that was Jerry. About ten minutes later, the doorbell rang. Naturally, she went to answer it, trying, as she reached for the knob, to figure out who could possibly be at the door at that hour. The door opened, she looked out—and then down. "Jerry! What are you doing here? How did you—what—why?" Sputter, sputter. He had climbed out the window and walked around outside to ring the bell to surprise her. Why did he do it? Because he could, that's why.

There are other family stories about the little devil. One concerns a billboard at the end of our block in Brooklyn—a real tall one, so tall that a ladder was built into its framework. When Jerry was about four, my parents found him at the top of it. And my aunt told me Jerry was banned from a neighborhood supermarket because he loved to take the bottom can out of displays to see if the display would remain standing without it. Sometimes it did, and sometimes it didn't. Some might say he was exercising his scientific curiosity. Those of us who lived with him had other words for it—or were rendered speechless.

Jerry was always a deep thinker and an observer of human nature, not to mention a practical jokester. You know the Looney Tunes cartoon with a devil on one shoulder and an angel on the other? That was Jerry. But where I was concerned, the devil usually won. I was, after all, the little sister, and Jerry was very much the older brother. It was his absolute obligation to torture me, but only when the mood struck him, and never when I expected it. It would have been no fun for him if I could predict what he would do to me, or when. That having been said, as Jerry got older, he and I got along very well together. That is, if you can overlook his throwing tacks on the floor when I was walking around barefoot. And if you can overlook his stapling my leg.

Since Jerry's death, I've been wondering why he did things like that. Was he just being mean? Never. That just wasn't his way, even as a child. Was it part of a game we were playing? Couldn't have been. We never played violent games. Neither of us was ever interested in that kind of play, and we're both pacifists at heart. So, after much thought, I think I now understand. Jerry was teaching himself the scientific method, and I was part of the experimentation process on two levels: First, did a stapler have enough power to pierce the skin and make a person bleed? Second, would I be stupid enough to let him do it? He seemed to gain affirmation from the first part: the stapler was strong enough to draw blood. And he seemed truly shocked at the second: I trusted him so completely that I allowed him to staple me. As I reflect on the event now, some sixty-odd years later, I think I'm kind of proud to have been one of his early science experiments. Proud, but permanently scarred. Even now I can see (or imagine I can see) those two little bloodspots that emerged from the staple piercing my flesh. But it all seemed so innocent then. Even now, I can't understand why I let him do the things I allowed him to do. Well, I guess I do understand. I never saw the devil in him. I just bled from the tacks and staples.

He was also the brother who would get into a quilt cover and pretend he was a dog, so I could be the dog's owner (for some reason, Jerry was Tootsie and I was Diane). Jerry played with me even though he didn't have to. He was often very thoughtful. When he went with his high school class to see a play in New York, he brought me back a Mister Peanuts plastic bracelet. I had it for about forty years. It was taken when our house was robbed, and its loss hurt more than losing the more expensive items. When our family moved to Long Island, Jerry decided one day to introduce our dog to the neighborhood, so he put a clown hat on our collie, Robin, and put him outside on the front stoop. Passersby were amused to see this huge dog dressed like something out of *Pagliacci*. That seemingly simple and innocent action should have warned the neighbors what to expect. But it didn't. When Robin died, I was distraught, so Jerry bought me a very strange but loveable dog named Champ. He had the looks of Lassie, but the intelligence of the Rock of Gibraltar.

Jerry was a real animal lover. When we took him to see Worcester Tech, before he actually applied there, we ran into a great deal of traffic at the Whitestone Bridge. Surprise. Traffic in New York City! Anyhow, as we sat there, Jerry saw a small dog running among the stopped cars on the bridge. Before anyone could stop him, he jumped out of the car and tried to grab the dog. Wouldn't you know it, the traffic started to move, and there was Jerry running among the cars in heavy Sunday night traffic trying to save some mongrel. Horns were blowing, cars were swerving, people were saluting Jerry with only one finger, and Jerry was oblivious. He just kept trying to coax the dog into our car. I'm sure that his failure to save the poor thing was something he always regretted.

Jerry and I were very close. When we took him to college to stay for the first time, my mom and I cried all the way home. I was very unhappy when he got married, not because he was getting married, but because he was going to California. I think I knew even then that he wasn't coming back East to live. While Jerry and his wife, Broni, were driving across the country on their honeymoon, he sent me a small ceramic collie. I still have it, although both it and I are a bit older, if not wiser. During his first year in California, Jerry missed all my senior year stuff in high school, including my graduation. To allay my disappointment, he promised me he would be with me for my birthday in August. He drove for three days straight and arrived just a couple of minutes before midnight, but still on my birthday.

Jerry also missed my college graduation, but I sort of forgave him for that because it was when his son, Keith, was born.

I have many memories of Jerry and family trips we took while we were growing up. After my son, David, and Jerry's children, Keith and Shannon, were born, we took trips to Washington, DC, to Lake Tahoe, and throughout California. When the kids were little, Jerry and his family would come East during the summer, with all four of their dogs, and stay for a long time. Those days are among my favorite lifetime memories.

As adults, the torture part of our relationship pretty much stopped, but the impishness, the joy in the joke, or, perhaps I should say the BOY in the joke, continued. On one of Jerry's trips East with his family, we all went on a religious pilgrimage to the Baseball Hall of Fame in Cooperstown, New York, a trip we had taken many times before. For Jerry, trips to Cooperstown ranked right up there with sharing thoughts with the Dalai Lama. For me, not so much. In fact, not at all. Anyhow, my son, David, shared Jerry's love of baseball, so all of us jumped into our eight-cylinder camel and headed off to Baseball Mecca. Along the way, we stopped at one of New York State's major tourist attractions, Howe Caverns. One part of the tour involves the lights being turned off so visitors may be shown how incredibly dark it is hundreds of feet down in a cave. Knowing Jerry, I should never have told him in the elevator that I was still uncomfortable in very dark places. Sure enough, when the lights went out, Jerry reached out and grabbed me, causing me to scream in fear and surprise. I think that shriek is still reverberating in that cave. Jerry never admitted grabbing me, but he never denied it, either. And he never ceased to remind me of it whenever we were in some dark place. That same day, we stopped for lunch in a greasy spoon. Shannon accidentally spilled some soda on David's jacket. We all laughed and that was that until later on, when David spilled some on Shannon's sweater. As I leaned forward to clean it up, I saw the gleam in Jerry's eyes as his hand moved toward his glass. "Don't you dare!" I warned him. His protestation of innocence was an Oscar-winning performance.

When Jerry became an adult, one childhood characteristic that he retained was his love of food. He used to love to come back to New York so he could pig out on the things he loved to eat, things that were almost all horribly unhealthy: Mrs. Stoll's knishes, Nathan's hotdogs, Wetson's hamburgers and Carvel ice cream. One time we were waiting for him at Kennedy Airport's baggage claim. His plane had already landed.

Ten minutes went by, then twenty, and finally a half hour had passed and no Jerry. He finally came down the ramp, wiping his face on a napkin. He had had to stop for a Nathan's hot dog—actually for six Nathan's hot dogs!

On that same trip, all of us stayed at our parents' house. My mother always baked Jerry's favorite stuff when he visited, and that trip was no exception. In search of an after-dinner snack, Jerry went into the kitchen to cut himself a slice of vanilla cake with fudge icing. I went in a short time later to get a drink and saw what he had done: he had eaten more than three-quarters of the cake! There was only one slice left.

On one of our rare trips West, Jerry took us to a cabin he had rented at Lake Tahoe, a place he dearly loved. Keith gave David a drink, and when David had finished it, Keith, with a grin, told him it was toilet water, directly from the toilet. Of course it wasn't really, but the look on Keith's face was pure Jerry. Of course, David chased Keith all around the house seeking vengeance, but what I most remember about the incident was the glow in Jerry's face as he and I both realized that the whoopee cushion had been passed to another generation of Waxmans.

As I think about and retell these incidents, I recall them with mixed feelings of pain and joy. It is the little things like these that make up MY Jerry, the simple man who enjoyed his family above all. It is said that brothers and sisters share a unique blend of love, camaraderie, and friendship. That is certainly true for Jerry and me. I loved him very much and miss him more than I can say.

Laura Waxman Ulric

Contents

Introduction

*J*erry Waxman died on October 13, 2009, after nine years of living with and fighting against Multiple Systems Atrophy. As Jerry put it, MSA "is not a nice disease." He wrote most of the pieces in this collection, *Playing on the Roof*—thirteen personal essays and two science fiction stories—during his illness. Only two, "Solar Eclipse" and "Sarsens," were written earlier. Jerry originally wrote "Sarsens" under the pseudonym, Max Dubinsky. It is published here under his own name. I don't think he will mind.

Friends encouraged Jerry to write about his illness, but he never did. Instead, he fashioned funny and tender stories about growing up in Brooklyn and Long Island, his passion for baseball and the Giants, his interest in girls, his brushes with death and with the law, and his love affair with solar eclipses. Rather than convey the experience of dying, these stories embody the wonder and joy Jerry found in living. This wonder is captured in the Preface of his book *Astronomical Tidbits*, published in 2010:

> I believe . . . [there is] . . . a fundamental reason why we look at the sky with wonder and longing—for the same reason that we stand, hour after hour, gazing at the distant swell of the open ocean. There is something

like an ancient wisdom, encoded and tucked away in our DNA, that knows its point of origin as surely as a salmonid knows its creek. Intellectually, we may not want to return there, but the genes know and long for their origins—their home in the salty depths. But if the seas are our immediate source, the penultimate source is certainly the heavens . . . . The spectacular truth is—and this is something that your DNA has known all along—the very atoms of your body—the iron, calcium, phosphorus, carbon, nitrogen, oxygen, and on and on—were initially forged in long-dead stars. This is why, when you stand outside under a moonless, country sky, you feel some ineffable tugging at your innards.

"We are star stuff," Jerry reminded us. "Keep looking up."

Jerry was a gifted teacher, and he continued to teach for as long as he could. When he could teach no longer, he focused on his writing. True to the pattern of his life, this pilot, skier, runner, hiker, painter, teacher and baseball fan pushed himself to do as much as he could for as long as he could. After his illness took hold, he continued to walk for as long as he could walk, although he often fell, hurting the wall, the furniture or himself. When he could walk no longer, he used an electric wheelchair, set to warp speed, and became an even greater danger to the walls and furniture. A great talker, Jerry talked with family and friends for as long as he could talk, and, as the reader will see from this collection, he was, and remained, funny. When he could talk no longer, he used an alphabet card to spell out words. "Been to any games lately?" An eater of sometimes heroic proportions, Jerry ate for as long as he could eat, and when he could barely swallow, family and friends kept him in egg creams and milkshakes, New York cheesecake and chocolate. Much of Jerry is in the pieces of this collection. In many senses, he spent his life playing on the roof.

In his last months, Jerry lay in a room watching movies and ballgames with family and friends, surrounded by many of his favorite things: family photos, a large framed photo of Bobby Thompson's 1951 homerun ("The Shot Heard 'Round the World"), a photo of Willie Mays's 1954 World Series catch ("The Catch"), a photo of himself sitting on the ancient stones at Stonehenge under a full moon ("Sarsens"), and a Tribble, a creature only Star Trek fans will recognize and emblematic of his love of science fiction.

This book is a labor of love by Jerry's friends and colleagues, among whom I count myself. As Jerry often said, with a twinkle in his eye, usually after eating a third piece of cheesecake, "It had to be done." The writing is all Jerry's; any errors in copyediting are mine.

Naneene Van Gelder
March, 2011

The Shot Heard 'Round the World

*O*ne day my grandfather came to me and said, "It's time you went to a baseball game. Get your jacket." The year was 1950; I was nine years old. I lived with my mother, father and sister in the Flatbush section of Brooklyn.

We climbed into his car and drove through Prospect Park to the Bedford Avenue side, parked and walked a few blocks to a large building that had the words "Ebbets Field" emblazoned on its side. After purchasing tickets, we walked into the darkened building and up a long, shadowed winding ramp. In the distance, at the end of the ramp, was a rectangle of daylight. As we approached the rectangle, our echoing footsteps gave way to a dull roar. It sounded as though on the other side of that rectangle I would see a waterfall—perhaps Niagara, which was the only waterfall I knew. When I stepped into the light, however, what I saw was more wonderful than any waterfall. What I saw changed my life forever. The field was gigantic—larger than anything I had seen before. And the color—before that moment, I did not know what "GREEN" meant. From that moment forward, that field is my definition of the word. It was pure magic. I was stunned. I was speechless. I was in love.

The game itself did not diminish my enthusiasm. Everything that happened served to excite me more: every hit, every fly ball, every ground ball, even every out. I was hooked, filleted and fried. The Dodgers beat Pittsburgh 5-2 that day, but I didn't care. It was the game that mattered. That wonderful game.

In the car, on the way home, my grandfather said to me, "Have you picked a team to root for yet?"

"Why?" I asked.

"Everyone has a favorite team," he replied.

"Well, I guess I'll root for the Dodgers," I said tentatively.

"If you want," my grandfather said, frowning. "But your father and I root for the Giants."

"OK," I recanted. "I'll root for the Giants too." Then, after a pause, "What are the Giants?"

"They are the team that plays in New York. The Dodgers are the team that plays in Brooklyn. And the Yankees are the team that plays in the Bronx." I rode home the rest of the way in silence. Had I made a mistake in committing to root for a team so far away? What would my friends say? I was worried . . . and I should have been.

My friends were merciless when they found that I had become a Giants fan. They berated me. They taunted me. They called my manhood into question. I was miserable, and I blamed my father and grandfather. The saving grace was that it was near the end of the season, so calm soon returned.

During the off-season, I flirted with changing allegiances but pride kept me from doing so. I refused to be pressured.

As the 1951 season started, it seemed that I had made a big mistake by remaining faithful to the Giants. They lost opening day. They lost their second game. They lost their third game. And they kept on losing. Five in a row. Eight in a row. Ten in a row. Eleven in a row. They started the 1951 season, my first full season of interest, by losing the first eleven games. My friends were ecstatic. I was miserable.

As the season progressed, it got worse. By the eleventh of August, the Giants found themselves 13½ games behind the Dodgers in the race for the National League Pennant—an almost impossible situation.

And then the team started winning. Two in a row. Four in a row. Six in a row. The Giants won sixteen games in a row, but even more importantly, they cut the Dodger lead to five games. From that day until the end of the regular season, the Giants played at a miraculous 37-7 clip, while the Dodgers played at a respectable 26-22 rate. The two teams finished the season in a dead tie.

In those earlier days of baseball, it was rare to have a tie at the end of a season. An exhausting 154-game schedule saw to that. But if two teams did manage to finish in a tie, the solution was a best two-of-three playoff (today, a single game decides in the event of a tie). In the city, there was no other possible topic of conversation. The streets were alive with anticipation. I, being a novice fan, took this unprecedented situation as perfectly normal. After all, I was ten years old. What did I know? I was totally unaware of the fact that only twice before 1951, once in 1946 and again in 1948, had a playoff game been necessary to decide the pennant winner. In 1946, the St. Louis Cardinals beat the Dodgers two games to none in the very first playoff series, and in 1948 the Cleveland Indians beat the Boston Red Sox in a one-game playoff. (The American League has always used a one-game playoff and the National League has since gone to that rule.)

Several factors made the current situation special. First, you had the Giants playing the Dodgers. Two more bitter rivals did not exist. Families were torn asunder and lifelong friendships were terminated because of the ongoing rivalry.

Second, the ferocity of the Giants' closing surge had set the baseball world on its ear. On the Giants' side, they had fought and struggled from so far back that they couldn't imagine being denied the pennant at the eleventh hour. On the Dodgers' side, they had just given up one of the largest leads in baseball history to their hated rivals. They didn't want to be saddled with the epitaph of the Worst All-time Choke.

The first game of the 1951 playoff was played on October 1st at Ebbets field in Brooklyn. The Giants won the contest 3-1 when Bobby Thomson hit a two run homer off relief pitcher Ralph Branca. Then the series moved to the Polo Grounds where the Dodgers won the second game 10-0 behind a complete game effort by rookie pitcher Clem Labine. The situation could not have been staged more dramatically.

The second game was played on a Sunday. There were rain showers that day, and I had been caught in one of them while playing ball. I remember being soaked to the skin and getting a chill in the late afternoon of that early October day. The next morning, October 3rd, I awoke with a sore throat. My mother decided that I would stay home from school. I didn't object because that way I could listen to the game on the radio. So, thanks to a lucky sore throat, I heard every pitch as Russ Hodges announced what was to become the most dramatic game in the history of baseball.

Pitching that day for the Giants was Sal Maglie. Nicknamed "The Barber" because of the close shaves he gave opposing players, Maglie had no love for the Dodgers, and Giants fans loved to see him on the mound against "dem bums." He had a career year in 1951, winning 23 games. His opponent was to be big Don Newcombe, the ace of the Dodgers, who matched Maglie sneer for sneer in meanness. It was the perfect match, for every pitch was dripping with hatred and the potential for mayhem.

The Dodgers drew first blood in the opening frame when Jackie Robinson singled home Pee Wee Reese. From there the game settled down to a series of goose eggs until the seventh, when Bobby Thomson tied the score by driving in Monte Irvin with a sacrifice fly. My cousin Neal, a Dodger fan, came to visit me in the bottom of the seventh and stayed for half an inning. But when Thomson drove in Irvin, he departed. The pressure was just too much for him.

Now the long season was beginning to show on both pitchers. First Maglie gave up three runs in the top of the eighth. Then, as the game headed into the bottom of the ninth with the Dodgers sporting a secure 4-1 lead, Newcombe showed signs of the overuse he had sustained in the final days of the season. Pitching on only two days rest and tiring badly, he attempted to take himself out of the game, only to have Jackie Robinson talk him into trying to finish the inning.

Shortstop and team captain Alvin Dark was the first batter. He started the rally with a single to center. Don Mueller followed with a single to right, sending Dark to third. With the tying run at the plate the ballpark started stirring.

I too, feeling the tension, took a favorite position in bed, on my back upside down with my legs extending vertically up the wall, reaching for the ceiling. The strain was becoming too much. The whole season was coming down to a finer and finer point.

Up to the plate strode Monte Irvin, the National League leader in RBIs. If the Giants were going to do anything, it had better be now. But Irvin, uncharacteristically anxious, went after the first pitch and popped out. You could feel the energy level drop in the park. One down.

However, not to be denied, first baseman Whitey Lockman shot a double down the left field line scoring Dark and sending Mueller to third, where he injured himself while sliding. Although we didn't know it at the time, Mueller had broken his leg in that slide. Clint Hartung was sent in to pinch run for him.

With slugger Bobby Thomson coming to the plate and rookie Willie Mays on deck, Dodger manager Charlie Dressen had little choice but to remove the beleaguered and spent Don Newcombe. Because he had no fully-rested pitchers, he decided to go with Branca, even though he had given up several home runs to Thomson that year, not to mention the "dinger" in game one of the playoff series.

Branca's first pitch to Thomson was a fastball strike on the outside corner. His second pitch, his last pitch of the season and the one he has had to agonizingly relive in the more than half century since he threw it, was a fastball high and inside. The pitch was designed as a set-up pitch for his next offering—a curveball down and away. But the pitch never reached catcher Roy Campanella's mitt. Instead Thomson yanked the fastball in a high arc toward the Polo Grounds' inviting left field stands, a mere 279 feet distant. As Dodger left-fielder Andy Pafco helplessly watched, the ball disappeared into the ridiculously close left field upper deck. What followed next was pure pandemonium, not only at the ballpark but in neighborhoods all over the city. In a microsecond my mood went from dejected fatalism to sheer, impossible joy. I leapt from my bed and ran screaming through the house, looking for someone to tell of the miracle that had just occurred in my bedroom. I found my mother sitting on the front porch with neighbors. Someone had a radio, turned loud, and they, too, were listening to the play-by-play that I had abandoned in my bedroom. Five or ten people, some of them passers-by, had walked up and onto the porch, attracted by the drama.

As Russ Hodges voice came screaming with delight out of the speaker—*"the Giants win the pennant and they're going crazy, they're going crazy! Ohhhhh-oh!!! . . ."*—there was, seemingly, one universal response—bewilderment and disorientation. Those who were sympathetic to the Dodgers were speechless, dumbfounded. How could this have happened? their eyes silently asked. And at the hands of the Giants, their worst enemy. And the Giants fans—well, they, too, were speechless and dumbfounded because they were not used to their Giants winning the crucial game. You see, I later learned, Giants fans of the last half of the 20th Century had a little bit of an inferiority complex. Why? Because deep down, way down in their heart of hearts, they knew that the Dodgers were the better team. I think that this is why, in the days that followed, I did not razz my friends, as they certainly would have done to me if the situation had been reversed. I knew that what happened in the game was a wee bit unfair, as the better team lost. Yes, I did celebrate when I was in the safety of my family circle, but I shared the grief of my friends when I was with them.

And, as it has turned out, I'm not so sure that the event was the best thing for my ten-year-old psyche. As I have mentioned before, being so new to the game, I did not know what to expect, what was rare or what was usual. I was surprised when the Giants lost the World Series to the Yankees. I thought it was a fluke. Rather, the fluke was Thomson's home run and the 1951 pennant race.

What I didn't know was that the Giants were on the brink of one of the longest droughts in major league history. True, they did win it all in 1954 when they swept the Cleveland Indians in the World Series, but that was the last time. They haven't won a World Series since. * During most of those years, their fans have had to go through lackluster seasons. When they have had a good team, they always seem to find some exasperating way of shooting themselves in the foot.

Some teams, like the Chicago Cubs or (until recent years) Boston Red Sox, have not won a World Series within memory. I think that is a kindness to their fans, and I think it's why Cub fans are generally considered nice people. They have not given their fans false expectations.

But I was not so lucky with the Giants. They took an impressionable youth and, albeit unintentionally, built his hopes to an unreasonable level. And they did this by winning, with what has come to be called "The Shot Heard 'Round the World" in the season known as "The Miracle at Coogan's Bluff."

The CALL

The main reason the WMCA call was recorded and saved for posterity was because a Dodger fan sought to torture a friend who was a Giants fan by capturing and replaying Russ Hodges's heartbreak from what he expected was going to be a Giants' loss. Only a tiny minority of people actually heard the

---

* Jerry wrote "The Shot Heard 'Round the World" in 2002. In 2010, a year after his death, the Giants did win the World Series. His friends think he may have played a role. (Ed.)

Hodges call live. Most heard Gordon McClendon's call on the Liberty Radio Network, which was carrying the game nationally. McClendon's account (complete with a similarly hair-raising yell of "THE GIANTS WIN THE PENNANT!") remains the only complete broadcast account of the third game.

This is what I, lying on my bed with my feet propped up against the wall, heard over the radio at 3:58 p.m. on October 3, 1951:

> *Bobby Thomson up there swinging . . . He's had two out of three, a single and a double, and Billy Cox is playing him right on the third-base line . . . One out, last of the ninth . . . . Branca pitches . . . Bobby Thomson takes a strike call on the inside corner . . . Bobby hitting at 292 . . . He's had a single and a double and drove in the Giants' first run with a long fly to center . . . Brooklyn leads it 4-2 . . . Hartung down the line at third, not taking any chances . . . Lockman with not too big a lead at second, but he'll be running like the wind if Thomson hits one . . . Branca throws . . .*

> *There's a long drive, it's gonna be, I believe . . . **THE GIANTS WIN THE PENNANT!! THE GIANTS WIN THE PENNANT! THE GIANTS WIN THE PENNANT! THE GIANTS WIN THE PENNANT! Bobby Thomson hits into the lower deck of the left-field stands! The Giants win the pennant and they're going crazy, they're going crazy! Ohhhhh-oh!!!"***

Playing on the Roof

NEW YORK TIMES, August 11, 1954—Two thirteen-year-old Brooklyn boys were killed yesterday when they fell six stories down the incinerator shaft of their Ocean Parkway Apartment house. Albey Reiner and Jerry Waxman, 7th grade students at Montauk Junior High School, were playing on the roof at 120 Ocean Parkway . . .

*O*ften, events do not register their significance at their moment of occurrence. They happen, are noted, and are relegated to the pile of the past, their potentiality summarily dismissed, their "might have been" ignored as a "never could be." As humans in an unforgiving world, we might argue that it's a waste of time, perhaps even counterproductive, to sit and ponder the unfulfilled eventualities of every incident. Yet there are often great and important lessons to be learned by looking carefully at events that did not happen.

It was August 10th, the day before Albey's Bar Mitzvah. Albey and I had been close friends for the past eight years, since kindergarten, and rarely did things without one another. Albey was born exactly one month to the day after I was, so his Bar Mitzvah came right on the heels of mine.

Now Albey is the most intelligent person that I have ever known. Not only was he always at the top of our class in school, but he also had a certain worldly wisdom. I always felt safe when I was with him because, whatever the situation, he would have the right slant on it. It was comforting. Naturally, Albey was also a whiz at Hebrew. As his Bar Mitzvah approached, I noticed no signs of nervousness or trepidation on his part; everything seemed under control.

This day in August was a typical warm summer Friday in the city. I woke at my usual (for the summer) 9:00 a.m., dressed in my usual jeans, striped, short-sleeved polo shirt and Keds and ate my usual breakfast of hot oatmeal. I left the house and headed toward Albey's. I walked south on East 5th Street and turned left at Caton Avenue. One block further was Ocean Parkway, and a left there brought me in sight of Albey's building.

In Brooklyn, Ocean Parkway runs from Park Circle at Prospect Park, south to Coney Island. The Parkway is about six miles long, and giant, brick apartment houses line most of it. City ordinances limit the height of these apartment houses to six stories, and lack of imagination limits their shapes to monotonous rectangular solids—red building blocks, neatly arranged side by side, all the same height, all the same color, all the same design—a Monopoly board come to life. The main distinguishing characteristic claimed by any of these structures was the number stenciled above each entrance.

As I walked toward 120 Ocean Parkway, I thought of how, just a few Fridays ago, I had been wracked with fear at my impending rite. The world was dark and dangerous in July, but now, in August, all was well.

I jumped on the elevator, rose to the 6th floor and walked to the door of Albey's apartment. Before I could even reach the door, it opened and out he sprang with his mother at his heels. "Where are you going?" she demanded. "Out to play ball," he replied. "Stop!" she shouted. Brought up short, Albey came to a halt, facing me, his back toward her, rolling his eyes in silent frustration. "What?" he asked, putting as much edge on his voice as he dared?

"You're not going out to play ball!" (firmly)

"Why not?"

"Because tomorrow is your Bar Mitzvah and I don't want you hurting yourself."

"I won't hurt myself."

"You're not playing ball!" (very firmly)

"I'll be careful."

"You're not playing ball!" (hint of anger)

"I want to."

"You're not playing ball!" (definite anger)

(pause: Albey knew when it was time to quit.)

"What can we do then?"

"Play nicely."

"What can we do?"

"I don't know what you can do. Find something to do."

"Can we play on the roof?"

"If you don't hurt yourself."

"OK (resignation), we'll play on the roof."

We were not strangers to the roof of Albey's building. Six stories up, the roof had attracted our attention years ago. When we discovered that the door to the roof was never locked, it became the place that we would go to look out over the city to watch the Tuesday night summer fireworks which took place six miles away in Coney Island or to have a Spauldeen catch with someone six stories below on the ground. Another favorite pastime was to sit on the bunker and watch them play ball at the Parade Grounds several blocks away.

The bunker was a low brick structure adjacent and attached to the rectangular chimney that vented the apartment's incinerator. The incinerator was located in the basement, and its chimney stretched upwards six stories to pierce the roof and extend an additional fifteen feet into the air. The chimney was rectangular, about six feet on a side and made of red brick. The bunker was a windowless, rectangular structure about ten by fifteen feet wide and six or eight feet high. It had a flat, concrete roof.

We had discovered that if we climbed onto the roof of the bunker, we could sit with our backs against the chimney and watch the happenings at the Parade Grounds. This was about as high as we could get, and it was our favorite way to pass time when nothing else more exciting was available.

Disappointed that our ball-playing plan had been thwarted, we bounded up the steps to the roof, ran across its tar and gravel surface to the chimney and climbed onto the bunker by first stepping onto an adjacent low brick wall. We sat down on the roof with our backs against the chimney and proceeded to scan east Brooklyn, the Parade Grounds and beyond to Long Island where, although I didn't know it at the time, I would be moving in one year.

I do not remember the precise conversation of that day. It most likely concerned (in order of probability) baseball, coins, the latest songs on the song sheet (we had discovered that one could buy a sheet that had the words of the top songs of that week; we would buy these sheets and memorize the words to the songs which, for whatever reason, seemed funny) or "the girls."

In had only been one year since "the girls" became a possible topic of conversation. Before the 6th grade, although they were always around and although (as we later admitted to one another) we thought about them a lot, coolness demanded that we treat them as pariahs who we shunned physically as well as in conversation. In the 6th grade, however, that all changed and we started attracting into loosely bound pairs, whose stability was constantly threatened by the still lingering, and to some degree socially induced, aversion which had been our prior masquerade. In any event, whatever the conversation might have been, we sat there enjoying the fine summer day and looking out over the city of Brooklyn.

After a brief time, I noticed a curious thing. The concrete slab that was the roof of the bunker, and upon which we were sitting, was criss-crossed with fine cracks that gave the surface the appearance of a jig-saw puzzle. I had never noticed this before and, for some reason, it interested me. I stood up and started walking around on the bunker roof, examining the cracks and speculating to Albey about their origin and meaning.

Even at this early age, it was clear to us that we were going to be scientists, so speculations into the nature of things were always in order. It was rare for us not to analyze situations, events and, without doubt, natural phenomena. We would spend hours discussing the structure of the universe (which as far as we knew, at that time, consisted of the sun, nine planets and about five hundred stars). Since one of us had recently been given an Earth globe, we had developed an interest in geography and would pass time with the globe and an atlas looking up places by their latitudes and longitudes. We were ripe with curiosity and transfixed by the ability of scientific inquiry to answer our questions.

Engaging in scientific speculation and having been Bar Mitzvahed, however, is no guarantee against grossly stupid behavior, especially if you're thirteen years old. There, on the top of the bunker, speculating about the nature and origin of the cracks, I decided to conduct an experiment. I decided to see if I could generate more cracks, or at least enhance the existing cracks, by stomping on the roof. Without hesitation, consideration, concern or trepidation, I walked to the center of the roof and started stomping with one foot. Nothing happened, so I stomped a little harder. Still, nothing happened. The cracks looked as they had before. Not discouraged, I started jumping up and down on the roof, stomping as hard as I could with both feet.

At this point, Albey, having considerably more sense than I, retreated to the corner of the roof, as far from the center as he could get. I, now furiously engaged in my experiment of destruction, had no knowledge that he had moved to a safe place. Had I seen him do this, I might have wondered why, and I might have come to the conclusion that my actions carried with them some element of danger. I might have stopped to ask him where he was going. I might have considered what was supporting this roof. I might have wondered what was under this roof. I, however, did none of these things. I neither wondered nor considered nor stopped; I just kept stomping.

The cave-in was instantaneous; its only depression in time was punctuated not by sight or sound (I remember neither) but by my stomach rising high in my chest, threatening to cut off my quick involuntary breath. At one moment my feet were in the air, gleefully propelling themselves downward in anticipation of the next mighty stomp at the heart of my concrete adversary; in the next, I was engulfed in total darkness.

The fall of about eight or ten feet resulted in an unexpectedly soft landing. The only light I could see was coming from above, and that light was dimmed by a blackish, fog-like mist in the air. My next breath told me that the mist hanging in the air was actually smoke or soot. It smelled as though I were standing in the remains of a dead campfire.

I couldn't quite see my feet, for my impact on the ground had raised a cloud of soot that had spread, knee high, across the entire surface of the floor on which I was standing. I could, however, feel that the floor was very soft; the ash into which I had fallen seemed about six inches deep. It was this that had broken my fall.

The smell was getting more intense as the rising ash entered my nose. My initial curiosity at my situation now took on an edge of alarm. How high would this "smoke" get? How was I going to get out of here?

"Are you OK?" I looked up, away from the darkness of the chamber and could see Albey's head silhouetted against the brightness of the blue sky. He was eight to ten feet above me, perched on a narrow outcropping of concrete which, miraculously had not caved in. He wasn't laughing. "You putz! You jerk! You broke it!"

"I've got to get out of here," I replied. "It's getting hard to breath. How am I going to get out?"

"Is there anything you can stand on? Look around in there."

I started bumbling around in the interior of the chamber, straining my eyes to see into the darkness, frantically looking for something on which to stand so that I might climb out of this pit. As I moved, I raised small clouds of soot which rose into the air a foot or so and then fell back to the ground. As my eyes grew more accustomed to the darkness, I began to see my trap more clearly. There were thick layers of soot everywhere. The dark, noxious substance covered not only the floor but also the walls and what little remained of the concrete ceiling.

"What is this place?" I said to Albey who was still peering down on me from his concrete perch. "I don't know," he replied, "but you'd better get out. We're going to get into trouble!"

I was now starting to be able to see quite well, and as I approached the far corner of the chamber, the corner I had been farthest from when I landed, I noticed a strange, square depression in the surface. It wasn't actually a depression so much as it was a place where the surface was darker. As I started to probe it with my foot, I realized that this depression was actually a square hole in the floor about two feet on a side. I pulled my foot back, immediately sensing the danger, and cautiously looked down into the hole. I could see about ten feet down into the shaft, the illumination coming from the sky above. Beyond ten feet, the shaft continued an unknown distance downward.

At that moment, I understood what this place was and how close I had come to killing myself. The bunker on which Albey and I had been sitting was a structure designed to capture soot and ash before it could escape into the Brooklyn air. The chimney from the incinerator six stories below extended through one corner of the bunker and then another ten feet upward. That hole into which I was now peering was a shaft sixty feet deep, terminating in the incinerator. Had I headed in the direction of the hole before the dust had settled or before my eyes had adapted to the darkness, I could easily have fallen in, and my end would have come 1.94 seconds later as I hit the ground at 42 miles an hour.

"Wow, look at this," I said to Albey, who was peering down from immediately above my head. "I could have fallen in!"

"What is it?" he asked.

"There's a hole here, and it looks like it goes all the way down to the basement." As I looked up at him, relaying this information, I realized that the peninsula of concrete on which he was standing was immediately over the hole. Had that piece given way when the roof collapsed, Albey would have fallen directly into the shaft. Albey must have had the same realization, for he quickly backed off the outcropping away from the lip of the cave-in and circled around to the other side of the hole.

"Maybe you can climb out if I help you," he suggested as he knelt, extending his arm downward. I slogged over to where he was and, stretching as high as I could, grabbed onto his hand. He tried to pull me out, but I was too heavy. "I can't do it alone," he said. "You'll have to help!" I put my foot on the wall and tried to climb up the wall while he pulled. But the side of the wall was thickly coated with soot and my feet kept slipping off. Because of all my activity, a black cloud of soot had started to form. "Wait a second," I said. "I have to make a toehold." I started kicking at the wall, trying to make a depression in the caked-on soot so that I could get a footing. The cloud of noxious black was rising waist-high now. "OK, let's try again," I said. For a third time Albey's arm came toward me, Sistine-like, out of the sky, and for the third time he pulled. This time it almost worked. With Albey pulling and me using the depression in the soot as a toehold, I was able to touch the lip of the roof before the caked-on soot gave way under the weight of my body. Again I fell back into my black prison—only now the cloud was chest high. Now I was really getting scared. If I didn't get out of there soon, that cloud was going to be head high, and I knew that I would not be able to breathe that stuff for long. I looked up at Albey. "What should I do?" I said, wetness coming to my eyes. "Try again," he said firmly. Again I kicked a toehold, and again an arm from heaven, and again the toehold broke. The cloud was now up to my neck. Within a minute it would engulf me. I looked up at Albey, silently, tears streaming. He looked at me firmly. "Again," he said. For the third time, I kicked a toehold.

The apartment houses that line Ocean Parkway were constructed in the 1930s as part of Roosevelt's plan to defeat the Depression. Construction companies under government contract would hire out-of-work men of all sorts to fill out their workforce. The apartment buildings that line Ocean Parkway were built by men who were, in their former lives, advertising executives, shopkeepers, teachers, landscapers. And they were good at their newfound work. Anyone who has been around these buildings knows that they are built to the highest of specifications. I, personally, am quite familiar with the quality of the bricklaying in these buildings. Formerly, I spent many years playing Chinese handball along the north side of 120 Ocean Parkway in Brooklyn. Now, as any Chinese handball player will tell you, you must have a wall free of imperfections to have any kind of reasonable game. By imperfections, I mean edges. Edges cause strange caroms, and caroms introduce a wild card into the game that, to the initiated, is intolerable. Obviously, in a brick building, the easiest way to get an edge is to have a brick out of position. Just one brick, either too far in or too far out and you have an edge. If you have an edge, you have a carom. If you have a carom, you have a problem—in Chinese handball. But the walls at 120 were perfect. Not one brick out of place—anywhere. Our Chinese handball games never had any do-overs.

Now, I have no idea what the frequency of mislaid bricks is at 120 Ocean Parkway, nor for that matter, anywhere else; I just know that it is very low. Yet when old 120 was under construction, one of the brick layers made a mistake. It wasn't a big mistake, but it was enough. Maybe he didn't notice it, but I think he did. Most likely he said to himself, "No one will ever see it up here," and he let it go. No matter how it happened, one of the bricks, in what from the outside appeared to be a perfect wall, was misplaced by about ¼ inch, so that it made a little ledge. When I kicked that third toehold, I kicked it about two inches above that ledge. When I put my weight on the depression in the soot and the depression gave way, as it had twice before and would have probably done forever, there was a different outcome. This time when the depression in the soot gave way, my foot slipped down a couple of inches and found the ledge that my benefactor had left for me some twenty years earlier. The firm purchase was all my young Keds needed. With me scrambling and Albey pulling, I managed to claw my way out of the chamber and onto the roof, which was nothing more than a rim of jagged concrete.

"Look at my arm!" Albey exclaimed. There, along a six-inch section of the inside of his forearm, were long bloody cuts and scratches.

"How'd you do that?"

"I scraped it on the concrete as I was pulling you out. Let's go downstairs and clean up."

Two minutes later we were standing in front of the door to Albey's apartment ringing the bell. I will never forget the look of horror on his mother's face when she opened the door. I was covered with black soot from head to toe. Carbon dust wafted from my body with my every move. It is likely that my own mother would not have recognized me. Albey, on the other hand was black only in the places where he had contacted me, most notably his hands. Blood, however, streamed from the cuts on his forearm.

"What happened?" she exclaimed.

"We need to clean up," Albey replied as he walked into the apartment. As I took a step forward to follow, Albey's mother barred my way. "Go home!" she commanded. "He needs to clean up," Albey called from inside the apartment. "He can clean up at home," she said as she stepped into the apartment and closed the door.

No one was home when I got there. I threw my clothes in the laundry bag and showered. When my mother asked me about the soot, I told her that Albey and I were playing in some ash. It wasn't until years later that I revealed the true story to my parents. By the time they knew about it, I was far too old to be punished. It was a good tactic.

I think about the event often—more often, the older I get. Had things happened in a slightly different way, Albey or I would have died that day and the long world lines that each of us has generated, along with their myriad nodes, leading to the perturbing and creation of other world lines, would not exist. In their place would have emerged an entirely different series of events and combinations of events that would have led to an entirely different universe from the one that occurred. Or, as some suspect, did the universe branch that day and double into a Siamese pair, joined at the moment of fall yet diverging from that instant into the one in which I now sit writing and another in which one of us died in 1954? I have no idea as to the answers to these questions, but I wonder.

As it was, Albey and I crossed into the universe that gave birth to our continued lives and this copy of the *New York Times*:

> *August 11, 1954—On an otherwise uneventful day, the Giants beat the Dodgers to take sole possession of first place in the National League. This is the first time that the Giants have occupied . . .*

Myles and Willie

$\mathcal{T}$ he torment started when we were young, seven or eight years old, and although it seldom became physical, we were completely cowed, with no thought of uprising or rebellion. We were abused not by our parents, not by our teachers, not by our siblings, and not by our neighbors. No, the instrument of our torture, like a north wind, swept down from the slopes of Greenwood Avenue as Genghis Khan from the Asian Steppes. The only difference was that our Mongol horde was a street gang that called themselves The Gremlins and was made up of boys who were no more than 10 years old.

I lived on the margin of a neighborhood that was middle class and mostly Jewish in the Flatbush section of Brooklyn. Traveling north from my house along East 5th Street, the first street that you came to was Fort Hamilton Parkway. This street served as the dividing line between my familiar, and therefore safe, neighborhood and the alien territory to the North—the territory populated by the toughs and the bullies. The demographic of the alien territory was Christian working class, but my friends and I just knew them as tough guys, or the toughs.

At the corner of East 5th Street and Fort Hamilton Parkway stood P.S. 130, my elementary school. It resided on the boundary between the two neighborhoods and provided the schooling for both. My friends and I would seldom, if ever, venture across Fort Hamilton Parkway into that Heart of Darkness . . . that is, unless accompanied by an adult. And the toughs seemed to understand that southeast of the Parkway was our territory. At least I don't remember their presence there, although no one, least of all we, would have stopped them if they had wanted to cross the boundary.

The point of contact between the two cultures was the playground of P.S. 130. When we were young, we did not have the run of the city as we did in later years. The only place for baseball was the schoolyard, so we would make tracks for it whenever we had the opportunity. The first thing that had to be done, however, was to send out a point man to check the schoolyard for toughs. If the yard was empty, we could play; if they occupied it, we were SOL.

The worst situation was when they showed up while we were already on the grounds and engaged in a game. The whole schoolyard was enclosed by a high chain-link fence that was breached by a gate in only one place along East 5th Street. If our enemies entered through the gate while we were already in the yard, we were trapped, and the torment would begin.

First, they would take our ball and refuse to give it back. Next, they would make us line up, get down on our knees and bow down to them. Then they would march us around, giving us strange orders. If any of us protested, they would threaten to beat us up. I never saw it come to that because we refused to stand up to them. We were cowards. They knew it. We knew it. It was humiliating but it was, we thought, just the natural pecking order. They were the wolves, and we were the sheep. Anyway, we knew that sooner or later we would leave this place for "the show," the big-time Montauk Junior High

School, which was far from P.S. 130 and far from the Gremlins. Things would certainly be better then—we thought.

Well, 1953 came and we graduated from P.S. 130. My family and I spent a great summer in a rented cabin on a lake in Yorktown Heights north of the city where I got my first: taste of nature, glimpse of the night sky, attempt at swimming, slice of pizza, kiss from a girl, and experience with kids who didn't live in Brooklyn. But the best part about being in Yorktown Heights was that there were no Gremlins.

At the end of August, full of myself, I returned to Brooklyn. I was excited at the prospect of going to this new school where the kids would certainly be more civilized than those we had to contend with from Greenwood Avenue.

Because we had to travel to school on public transportation, we went the first day with Robert Bauer, an 8th grader we knew from Albey's building. He had graduated from P.S. 130 the year before and, as such, was the reigning expert on Montauk. The trip to school was fairly easy, but far. We were accustomed to walking down the block to P.S. 130. That trip took less than a minute. Now we had to go to the bus stop on the corner of Caton Avenue and East 4th Street and take the bus to 13th Avenue and 42nd Street in Borough Park. From there we had to walk to 16th Avenue and 43rd Street where the school was located.

As the bus drove along 13th Avenue in Borough Park, it became more and more crowded with kids who were heading to Montauk. After a while, all the seats were taken. Then all the standing room disappeared. But they still kept coming, pushing in through both the front and rear doors (the driver had given up checking the Transit Authority bus passes we had been issued) until the bus was a sea of bodies. It appeared to me that the other kids enjoyed the chaos of the bus ride, but it unnerved me. It offended my sense of decorum and order. It felt . . . uncivilized.

At noon, all the kids in the 7th grade had their lunch hour. We shuffled down to the basement where the cafeteria was located and stood in the line that slowly moved parallel to the long, polished aluminum counters, behind which women in white dresses and aprons spooned an unidentifiable food-like substance onto plastic plates. The material was tasteless, so overcooked that all of its individuality had been vanquished. We weren't sure whether we were eating animal, vegetable, or mineral. On that first day we took a vow never again to eat the food/substance produced in that cafeteria.

The next day we decided to try our luck eating off school grounds in the mom and pop establishments that were ubiquitous in that part of the city. Walking along 42nd Street from 13th to 16th Avenue the next morning, we spied a bakery that sold pizza, three delicatessens that sold hot dogs and French fries, and a luncheonette that sold chow mein sandwiches. We were thrilled at the prospect of partaking of this gastronomic feast. When the noon bell rang, we made a beeline for the chow mein sandwiches that were made at the luncheonette, a mere fifty feet from the gate that separated the school yard from the public sidewalk.

As we approached the gate, it became clear that there was going to be a problem. There, barring our path, were about half a dozen unsavory looking characters of a type we were all too familiar with. They may not have been the Gremlins per se, but they were certainly of the same ilk. As we moved toward the opening in the fence, they moved to cut us off. When it became apparent that they were not going to let us pass, we stopped. One of them, a kid in a T-shirt, jeans, and rather high-heeled chukka boots, spoke first.

"Where ya goin'?" he asked in a mock-friendly voice. The kid was of medium height and weight, nothing to be afraid of physically. It was his eyes that were unnerving. They were half closed, as though he had just awakened from a deep sleep, and they ceaselessly darted from side to side, never coming to rest on a single subject, not even on the person their owner was threatening.

"Out to buy lunch," one of us answered innocently.

"Got any spare change?" Boots shot back. It wasn't so much a question as a demand.

I was shocked. This was the first time anyone had asked me for money. The thought that immediately popped into my head was, "Do I have enough money to share with this stranger?" I did a rapid calculation. I had $0.75. The menu I had planned for myself included:

> 1 chow mein sandwich at $0.25
> 1 bag of French fries at $0.15
> 1 slice of pizza at $0.20
> 1 pickle at $0.05
> 1 Carvel cone at $0.10

No, it was clear that if I were going to have my desired lunch, I had no spare change.

"No," I replied. "I have no extra change."

"Oh yeah?" said Boots. "Let's see." With that, two of Boots's companions grabbed me by my arms and pinned me to the fence while Boots rifled my pockets. I was so surprised and scared that I put up no resistance.

"What's this?" said Boots in mock surprise, as he pulled from their now, clearly, not-so-secure resting place, the three quarters my mother had given to me that morning.

"Holdin' out on us, huh," he said as he pocketed the quarters.

Apparently finished with me, Boots turned to my two companions. "What about you guys? Got any spare change to contribute?" Learning their lesson quickly, they each reached into their pockets, pulled out a handful of change, and dropped it into his outstretched hand.

"Thanks, boys," said Boots. "See ya tomorrow. And, by the way," he added, "if you tell anyone about this, you'll be sorry. I promise. Now get outta here."

As we beat our retreat, I looked back over my shoulder just in time to see Boots & Co. accost another small group of freshman-looking innocents. It looked to be a long two years at Montauk Junior High School.

The next day, I recounted the incident to some of my friends during our homeroom period. They informed me that Boots's real name was Willie Trumbull. He was a real bad character who was in the 7th grade for the third time. What's more, he had three older brothers who were worse than he was. Their advice: stay away from Willie!

As hard as it was to get past the hoods at the gate, it wasn't impossible, and even a small chance at a gourmet meal was better than the slop served at the cafeteria. At first we were intercepted about three times per week, but gradually we got better at avoiding interception or at hiding our money so that it wouldn't be found if we were frisked. The best way to escape detection was to let some other poor unsuspecting schnook run interference for us. We would hang back, out of sight of the gate and wait for someone to be accosted. Then, while the hoods were doing their thing, we would have a shot of getting through the gate without being noticed. Within three months, we were getting through 80% of the time. If we were caught, we were caught, and we meekly gave up our money. The thought of fighting back never occurred to us. Years of being bullied had conditioned us to passively submit. Then Myles arrived and everything changed.

It was the middle of November when Myles moved into the neighborhood. The first time I saw him was when our homeroom teacher, Miss Friedstein, walked into the classroom with this average-looking kid in tow. She walked to the front of the room and scanned up and down each aisle. When her eyes fell on me, she stopped and beckoned to me to come to the front of the room. When I reached her, she nodded at the boy at her side and said, "Jerry, this is Myles Derison. He's a new student here, and I'd like you to take charge of him for a few days. Show him around. Introduce him to your friends. And above all, keep him out of trouble!"

For the next few days I exercised my promise to Miss Friedstein. Before long, however, it became clear to me that I was hanging out with Myles not because of the promise but, rather, because he was fun to be around. He was congenial, bright and funny; was he ever funny. It seemed as though he was able to see the humorous (I would now call it ironic) side of any situation—or so I naively thought at first. However, I soon discovered that there were limits to his sense of humor.

The day after Myles arrived, we took him to lunch with us. We were on our way out of the schoolyard to get our chow mein sandwiches, and, as was our habit, we waited until Willie and his henchmen were preoccupied with the mugging of some other kid. At precisely the right moment, we made our break for the gate. The trick was to move quickly, quietly, nonchalantly, and, above all else, not to draw attention to ourselves. We had done it many times, and it worked. The only problem was that we had overestimated Myles's ability to pass by a person in distress. As we passed behind Willie, who was busily searching the pockets of some unnamed unfortunate, a voice called out.

"Hey, leave the kid alone!"

I froze in my tracks. I couldn't believe my ears. The voice was Myles's and he was standing next to Willie Trumbull, staring at him. Willie ceased his exploration of the kid's pockets and slowly turned toward Myles.

"What did you say?" he asked in a measured tone.

"I said leave the kid alone," Myles repeated.

I grabbed Myles by the arm and tried to pull him away and through the gate. "Are you crazy?" I hissed. But he pulled his arm from my grasp without looking at me. His gaze, unwavering, was still fixed on Willie.

A half-smile/half-sneer spread across Willie's face. "This kid was just giving us his spare change. Maybe you'd like to contribute some."

"I don't have anything for you," Myles shot back.

"Is that right?" countered Willie as he turned toward his gang of thugs who were leaning against the fence. "Let's see what you *do* have." Willie gave them some sort of signal, and in a flash, four of them were on him.

Unlike me, Myles fought back. There were no punches thrown—just a lot of pushing and shoving. Myles went down to the ground with the four attackers on top of him. They wrestled around on the pavement for about twenty or thirty seconds until, finally, he was pinned. They proceeded to go through his pockets until they found his change and relieved him of it. Then they got to their feet and walked toward Willie who had watched the exchange while leaning against the fence.

Myles continued to lie on the ground, breathing heavily. I walked over to him and bent down. His pants were torn, and I could see his bloody knee through the hole. A welt was starting to appear where his forehead had struck some hard object—probably the ground.

"Are you OK?" I asked.

"Yes . . . . No," he moaned.

I could see on his face a mixture of anger and embarrassment. I decided, for the moment, not to say anything to him about the incident. I helped him to his feet and, together, we walked back into the school. We didn't eat lunch that day.

On the way home from school on the bus, I talked with Myles about what had happened. I was amazed to discover that Myles had an entirely different slant on the bullies than I had. I had grown up being bullied. I was as accustomed to it as I was to air. It just came with the territory, so, as much as I could, I tried to ignore it. For Myles, however, the bullying was new, and he was outraged by it. "It's wrong and I'll never give in to them," he said to me at the end of our conversation. "Then you're gonna get your ass kicked," I replied. "I don't care," he said softly as though talking to himself. "I'll never give in."

From that day forward, Myles drew Willie's attention like a lightning rod draws electrons. Whenever Willie saw him, whether before school, at lunch, or after school, there would be a confrontation that always went the same way. Willie would ask Myles for his spare changed. Myles would refuse to give any up. Willie would turn his attendant Neanderthals on Myles who would, although he fought valiantly, be thrown to the ground and robbed. I can't imagine how many pairs of pants he went through.

In the next few weeks, the rest of us, those who didn't fight back, noticed an obvious reduction in our encounters with the hoods. I like to think that it was Myles's doing. I think that they concentrated their attentions on him, paving the way to lunch for the rest of us.

This went on from 1953 to 1955—our entire stay at Montauk. During that period, Myles and Willie remained locked in an orbit that now appears to me to have been symbiotic. It was as though each depended on the other to fulfill some unnamed need or desire. The psychology of the relationship was certainly beyond my understanding, both then and now.

When we left Montauk in 1955, Myles to go to Erasmus High School in Brooklyn and I to go to Valley Stream South High School on Long Island, I thought the Willie Trumbull story had ended. But it hadn't—not quite.

In 1975, twenty years after we left Montauk, I was living in Los Angeles and teaching at Santa Monica College while Myles was living in Spring Valley and working for an advertising firm in New York City. That summer, as was my habit, I was visiting my parents who, by this time, had moved to New Jersey. As usual, when I traveled East, I'd try to see Myles. This time, we decided to meet on East 5th Street and do the old neighborhood. We looked at our respective houses, walked the streets and took the bus to Montauk. We went into the school and inquired about our 8th grade homeroom teacher, Mr. Agolia. We tried to get a chow mein sandwich, but the luncheonette was no longer there. Nor were most of the other eating establishments we had frequented. Despite these disappointments, we had a great time.

Walking from Montauk, back up 42nd Street, toward the 13th Avenue bus stop, we were passing the old Borough Park Yeshiva, commenting that it appeared no different after all these years, when Myles pulled up short.

"Jerry, look!" he said, pointing to a car parked nearby. "Isn't that Willie Trumbull?"

The man in the car was sitting in the front passenger seat with the door open and the seat halfway reclined. His feet rested on the sidewalk, so he was half inside and half outside the car. His eyes were closed, and he appeared to be sleeping. Both he and the car were rather ragged, and the feet sticking out onto the sidewalk were encased in chukka boots. There was no doubt about it. Myles was right.

As we stood there whispering, Willie sleepily opened his eyes. It took him a few seconds to get his bearings. Then he looked at us quizzically. "Do I know you?" he asked. His speech was lightly slurred, as though he had been drinking.

"Yeah," Myles said. "We went to junior high school together."

"Oh," croaked Willie, as his head fell back on the seat and his eyes closed.

Myles and I just looked at one another and started walking toward the bus stop. We had gone less than five steps when we heard Willie call out.

"Hey," he said.

We both turned.

"Got any spare change?"

Again, Myles and I looked at one another, this time in wonderment. We started laughing as we turned once again toward the bus stop. This time we got maybe thirty feet before Myles stopped.

"Wait a minute," he said. He turned and walked back to Willie. When he got to the car, he reached into his pocket and pulled something out, which he handed to Willie. Then he walked back to me, and we continued toward 13th Avenue.

"What did you give him?" I asked.

"Ten bucks," he replied.

"You're kidding," I said. "What'd you do that for?"

A long moment passed as Myles analyzed his actions.

"For old time's sake," he answered.

We walked in silence to the bus. There was nothing more to say.

The Catch

*I*n 1954, I was thirteen years old. Summers were always the best time of year for me, but this one, like the spring tide, was destined to bring some of my highest highs as well as lowest lows.

The thirtieth of June was the magic moment for kids who lived in New York City, for it was on that day that school closed. For ten glorious weeks, the days were ours. For ten weeks we would not have to spend six hours a day sitting in regimented columns behind ancient wood and cast iron desks. For ten weeks we would not have to run to the deli across the street at lunchtime, hoping to get there to buy our chow mein sandwich lunches before we were accosted by toughs who would steal our nickels and quarters. For ten weeks there would be no homework at night, no French to practice, no algebra over which to puzzle, no Shakespeare, no lima bean biology, no Civil War. For ten weeks we could do whatever we wanted, and we all knew what that was: baseball.

On this topic there is no doubt whatsoever. Rational people would agree that the golden age of baseball took place during the 1950s in the city of New York. There were sixteen teams in major league baseball in those days (as God intended), but only three of them mattered. The Yankees, grudgingly admired as the greatest, were generally ignored until the seemingly inevitable September showdown when they would beat either of the two really important teams in the World Series.

Baseball was about the Giants and the Dodgers. It was defined by the Giants and the Dodgers—both in the same league, sharing the same city, dividing friends and families in more intense conflict than any political or religious question. From April until September, it seemed as though the city of New York existed only to act as a stage for the playing of the great Giant/Dodger drama. It gave our lives meaning. In fact, I can remember feeling sympathy for the unnamed millions of lost souls who lived in other places and did not have the thrill of being part of the New York baseball scene.

On summer days, we would meet in the schoolyard of P.S. 130 on the corner of Fort Hamilton Parkway and East 5th street and reconnoiter the ball field. If it appeared safe (i.e. if there were no toughs in sight) we could carry on our ball-playing there. If, as was often the case, the toughs were there, we would carry our equipment the few short blocks to the Parade Grounds at the head of Ocean Parkway. This seemingly infinite expanse of grass and playing fields did not have the advantage of outfield fences that our thirteen-year-old fly balls could reach, but it more than made up for the absence of fences by providing a multitude of grown-ups, which made harassment far less likely.

After a morning of ball playing came the really important games of the day, the games in which the Giants and Dodgers were playing. Generally, we would find a radio somewhere and listen to the unfolding of the contest. Often, we would continue our ball playing to the sounds of Red Barber's or Russ Hodges's play-by-play. On rare occasions, we would board the IND to the Polo Grounds or the BMT to Ebbets Field so that we could watch, in person, the gladiatorial event. The summer of 1954 was a good summer for my Giants and, therefore, a great summer for me. After the ecstasy of 1951, the Giants had fallen on hard times in '52 and '53. The reason, as everyone knew for sure, was that Willie Mays had been drafted into the Korean "conflict," and since he was the heart of the team, there was no way to expect too much until he returned. But then, my father assured me, things would be different. "Just wait until Willie returns!"

Well, in 1954 Willie returned and guess what? They were right! From day one of the season, when Willie won the game with a home run, the Giants bolted to the league lead. Willie was amazing; every day he made some new great play in the field or on the bases or at the plate. And when it wasn't Willie it was Mueller or Dark or Williams or some great pitching by Antonelli or Wilhelm. By early August, the Giants seemed assured of the pennant. At one point in late August or early September, the Giants played the Dodgers six times in two weeks—three times at the Polo Grounds and three times at Ebbets Field. And can you believe it, the Giants won all six! As a thirteen-year-old Giants fan in Brooklyn, whose friends were all Dodger fans, I was ecstatic.

I can remember to this day, more than half a century ago, the final out in the game in which the Giants clinched the pennant. As fate demanded, the magic number reached "2" on the day of a Giants-Dodgers game.[1] The score was 6-1 when the last Dodger batter hit a little tapper to pitcher Sal Maglie,

---

[1]   For the uninitiated, the "magic number" is the number of wins plus rival losses required for a team to clinch a pennant. In this case, the magic number was 2, meaning that 2 Giant wins would clinch the pennant. Two Dodger losses would do the same thing, as would a Giant victory combined with a Dodger loss.

who threw to first baseman Whitey Lockman for the last out of the pennant-clinching game.

Amazingly, the Yankees, perennial champions of the American League, did not win the pennant in 1954. Rather, it was the Cleveland Indians who came away with the crown. One might have surmised that that would have been a good thing as far as the Giants were concerned since the Yankees seldom lost a World Series, and they had beaten the Giants in the Fall Classic as recently as 1951. But the 1954 Indians were a superb team. They had, in that year, broken the record for wins in a season (111) and they were given the nod as the odds-on favorite to win the series. It looked to be another disappointing October for my Giants.

Game One of the 1954 World Series was played on September 29th at the Polo Grounds in New York City. Although no one knew it at the start of the game, the outcome of the match was going to be decided by more than the players on the field. The field itself was going to have the deciding vote as to who would be the victor.

I had developed a new habit during the 1954 season, a habit many people adopted that year. Instead of listening to the game on the radio, as I had in past years, I shifted my allegiance to the television. Now, I don't want you to think that I made lightly the decision to come over to the Dark Side. *Pas de tout!* Let me get this out, here and now. I think the radio is a lovely medium. Not only does it give the listener a chance to exercise his or her imagination, but also, in the early days of television, radio had the advantage of being able to take you to places that TV could only dream about matching. Ride with the Lone Ranger, fly with Sky King, mush with Sergeant Preston—radio could do it—TV could not. At least not in the early days. But baseball, TV could do. And it was almost like being there.

My father, grandfather, and two uncles sat with me, crowded around my grandparents' 16" screen. This was how I watched the first game of the 1954 World Series.

Now, everybody knows that baseball is a game of hitting, running, and catching. What is not so well appreciated is that baseball is also a game of words. Baseball has a lexicon that is laced with jargon and colorful metaphors, and while other sports have their own unique phrases, baseball's 160 years as an American sport insures a rich verbal tradition. In fact, as the span of time from the inception of a word or phrase gets longer, even the diehards may have difficulty remembering the origin. Take, for example, "dinger,"[1] "southpaw,"[2] or "Texas Leaguer."[3] How many people who are not baseball aficionados have heard of them or know what they mean?

Even players are tagged with colorful names, some loosely metaphorical, most nonsensical. These nicknames are signs of affection, or at least respect. Sometimes the better players have more than one nickname, the leader being, of course, George Herman Ruth with "The Babe," "The Bambino," "The Sultan of Swat," and "The King of Swing." Fans may also recognize "The Splendid Splinter,"[4] "The Say Hey Kid,"[5] and "The Man."[6]

---

[1] Dinger: A home run.
[2] Southpaw: A left-handed person. Generally, a pitcher.
[3] Texas Leaguer: A bloop single. A ball that has been poorly hit but falls in for a single anyway.
[4] The Splendid Splinter = Ted Williams of the Boston Red Sox.
[5] The Say Hey Kid = Willie Mays of the New York (later San Francisco) Giants.
[6] The Man = Stan Musial of the St. Louis Cardinals.

Aside from these nicknames, baseball abounds with obscure references to famous or infamous plays. For example, "The Called Shot,"[7] or "Merkle's Boner,"[8] or "The Shot Heard 'Round the World,"[9] or "The Catch." Now, it may seem strange that you can just casually say two words, "The Catch," to a group

---

[7] The Called Shot: Babe Ruth's home run off Charlie Root in the 5th inning of the 3rd game of the 1932 World Series, a home run which was said to have been hit after the Bambino pointed toward the center field bleachers, an action that some take as a prediction.

[8] Merkle's Boner refers to the mistake that New York Giants rookie first baseman Fred Merkle made in the 9th inning of the last game of the 1908 season. With the score tied, a runner on 1st and two out, Merkle singled to right field. The next batter, Al Bridwell, hit a single to center, which scored the base runner Moose McCormick. Seeing McCormick cross the plate, Merkle–as was the custom of the time in such situations–headed for the Giant clubhouse in center field. Cub second baseman Johnny Evers–a stickler for rules–noticed that Merkle had not gone on to touch second. Evers called for the ball, tagged second and appealed to umpire Bob Emslie who did not see the play and refused to make the call. He appealed to his partner, the famous Hank O'Day, who granted Evers's appeal and called Merkle out on a force play. The Giants had left the field, celebrating their victory when umpire O'Day declared the game a tie. When the game was made up on October 8th with the Giants and Cubs tied in the standings, the Giants lost the game—and lost the pennant.

[9] The Shot Heard 'Round the World: Bobby Thomson's walk-off home-run which won the third game of the 1951 National League Pennant for the New York Giants against their cross-town rivals, the Brooklyn Dodgers. The two teams had finished the 154-game season in a tie and were engaged in a best two out of three playoff series. The Giants won the first game and the Dodgers the second.

of baseball fans and they will know to what you are referring. I assure you, they will.[10]

You see, baseball is much more than today's game. Baseball is a game steeped in history, bathed in tradition. It is a game of records and numbers, streaks and statistics. It is a game of heroes and demagogues, a game wherein its most famous practitioner could almost certainly apocryphally point to the centerfield stands and have the story retold to the point where, three quarters of a century later, it is the stuff of mythology.

Many great moments illuminate the halls of the history of baseball. Two of these moments, one offensive and one defensive happened in games that featured the New York Giants, and as such, I had the good fortune to witness them. One, of course, is the story of the Amazing 1951 season of the New York Giants and of the third game of the 1951 National League Playoff series—the game that ended with The Shot Heard 'Round the World.

The other great moment was, given the circumstances, the greatest defensive play ever seen. Baseball fans call it The Catch, and it happened in the top of the eighth inning of the first game of the 1954 Word Series—the game that I was about to watch on my grandparents' 16" TV set.

The game was close through the first seven innings. The score was tied at two in the top of the eighth. Larry Doby led off with a walk, and Al Rosen singled him to second. Giants' manager Leo Durocher brought in reliever Don Liddle to face

---

[10] The Catch: Now some poor, misguided fools (generally football fans) have the silly notion that "The Catch" refers to catch that Dwight Clark made of the Joe Montana touchdown pass in the 1982 NFC Championship game. I assure you that they are wrong!

left-handed slugger Vic Wertz. Wertz ran the count to 2-1. On the next pitch he hit a monstrous blast to dead center. It was obvious from the crack of the bat that this ball had home run written all over it. But this ball had to contend with the Polo Grounds, the Giants' home field. This field was the most oddly shaped in the league: 258 feet down the right field line, 279 feet down the left field line, and 483 feet to center. In fact, only one person, Joe Adcock from the Milwaukee Braves, had ever hit one out at center.

So Vic Wertz's drive was not going to be a home run, not in the Polo Grounds, but it looked destined to fall on the grass between the center field wall and Willie Mays, who was running toward the fence for all he was worth, his back to home plate.

When the ball was struck my heart sank. This ball was surely going to be an extra base hit, scoring at least two runs. The ball was flying over Mays's head, and Mays was running full tilt for the center field wall. It seemed as though an eternity passed. Then time stood still. At the last instant Mays, still running, his number 24 still clearly visible to the TV camera, extended his arms forward and snatched the ball out of the air on the warning track. He applied the brakes, wheeled, and threw the ball to the cut-off man at second, holding the lead runner, Larry Doby, at third and saving a run. It was the most remarkable catch I have ever seen to this day, not only for the physical gymnastics required to pull it off but also for the high-pressure situation. In the stands there was a moment of disbelief as people assured themselves that they had really seen what they had just seen. Then the partisan crowd erupted in a mighty roar. The threat was over.

The score remained tied until the last of the ninth inning. There was one man on base when Giant manager Leo Durocher called on left-handed pinch-hitter Dusty Rhodes. Rhodes hit a pop behind first base—at least that is what it looked like. Right fielder Dave Pope started circling under the ball. The ball was caught in the wind, which always blows towards the right field fence late in the New York afternoon. Closer and closer to the right field wall Pope slid, but the ball dropped into the first row of the stands, 258 feet away from the plate—a 258-foot home run. It was the cheapest homer hit all year, but it won the first game of the Series for the Giants.

The Indians were stunned. The juxtaposition of a 258-foot home run with a 460-foot out was too much for them to take. I think that after Willie's catch and Rhodes's admittedly cheap home run, the Indians lost their heart and spirit. They promptly lost the next three games of the Series. In the end, the Giants won the Series four games to none against the team that not only had been favored to win but also had broken the American league record for wins during the season.

1954 was the last time the Giants won the World Series. The only team to have a longer drought is the Chicago Cubs. And so I wait and wonder if I will ever again in my lifetime witness events as glorious as those in my youth. As of late I have become somewhat jaded, so I think the answer is no. More and more I am beginning to believe that youth cannot be crossed with later years. That the events that occur when you are young are special because you are young, and they can never be duplicated. By this measure, The Catch is a myth, and as with all myths, it can never be duplicated in life. I hope I'm wrong.

The Lunchtime Express

I don't clearly remember how it started, but when we were in eighth grade, our second year at Montauk Junior High School, we got into the habit of taking buses and subway trains all over the city to see just how far we could travel during the noon lunch hour. The "we" I refer to are Myles Derison, Marty Wasserman, and myself. At the stroke of 11:56 a.m., when the bell rang signaling the end of the fourth period and the start of our lunch hour, we raced to our respective lockers to deposit our books, grab our jackets and lunches and rendezvous in front of the main office just inside the entrance to the school. We picked that meeting place because one of us had noticed that the hoods who accosted us and stole our money seemed to be magnetically repelled by the main office (perhaps because within was housed the principal); you couldn't find one within a hundred yards of the place on a bet. It wasn't so much that we minded being accosted and robbed by them; by this time we pretty much had them figured out and knew how to neutralize their effect. No, the reason we picked that meeting place was we were "on-the-clock," so to speak, and could leave promptly without dealing with their petty games.

We would grab our possessions and make a beeline for the bus stop or the subway station. There, we would board the first bus or train to show up (to anywhere) and ride until we felt that if we rode any longer, we would be late getting back. We would then keep a record of where we ended up and, using a map of Brooklyn, we would determine the distance we had traveled from school. The thing that made all of this possible was the New York Transit Authority passes given to us because we lived so far from Montauk that it would have been a financial hardship on our families for us not to have them. The only stipulation was that the passes, good for traveling on all of New York City's transit systems, be used for the legitimate transit from home to school. Needless to say, the ethics of our game never entered our minds.

One day, one of us said, "Gee, I wonder if we could get as far as Coney Island?"

"Wouldn't that be neat?" I said. "Maybe we could get a Famous." I was, of course, referring to Nathan's Famous hot dogs, a delicacy to all New Yorkers with well-developed palates.

The thought of the Famous pretty much sealed our decision to try for the prize. The first thing to do, of course, was make a back-of-the-envelope calculation to ascertain whether or not this was a reasonable quest. We used an old AAA map of my father's that showed it is only about five and a half miles, as the crow flies, from Montauk to Coney Island. Moreover, we had heard that a subway train travels thirty to thirty-five miles per hour. It doesn't take an algebra whiz to figure out that the train *could* make the trip in the allotted time.

However, those of us who know anything at all about the New York subway system know two things: One, the train is not a crow, and two, the line has stations—where you stop. In fact, the average speed of a NY subway train is between ten and eleven mph. When compared to the approximately eleven-mile trip we had committed ourselves to taking, you can see that it was going to be close.

As we rode along the Avenue stops leading to Coney Island, the subway train, acting out its name under much of the city, roared up above ground at Ditmas Avenue, there to remain elevated (or an "El" as the inhabitants call it) for the eleven stops that it makes to reach the end of the line at Stillwell Avenue in Coney Island.

While the train was underground, we calmly ate our lunch, watching the stations pass practically unnoticed. But as soon as we came above ground, the stops became much more obvious, bringing attention to my mistaken calculation. In five minutes, a timed stop and a second back-of-the-envelope calculation revealed the truth: it was too close to call. Whether or not we got back in time would depend not on the gross properties of the trip, those being the speed of the train and the distance to Coney Island. Those two variables canceled one another out, yielding the dead heat result. No, as with Chaos Theory, what was going to matter more were the little things—the things that you wouldn't ordinarily think would matter—such as how long the door remained open at a stop or how long a break the conductor took at the end of the line. Had we known that we were going to be putting our faith in such capricious hands, I don't think we would have attempted the trip. In fact, I don't understand why we just didn't turn around right then and there, why we didn't wait for a better opportunity. Maybe we figured that once we started on the quest, we were committed. Maybe it was machismo.

You have to understand that we were really performing a risky task, for the teachers and administrators at Montauk were strict. They had to be; they were dealing with a population of young hoodlums and thugs mostly and they knew, as every prison guard knows, that any sign of weakens or any kindness that could be taken for weakness was an invitation to disobedience. The fact that there was a small population of good kids mixed in with the delinquent elite was just too bad for the good ones; the rules had to be enforced uniformly across the board.

As we sped toward Coney Island, we kept a nervous eye on the time. The start of the lunch hour was 11:56. The bell marking the end of lunch and the beginning of a short homeroom period, during which attendance was taken, rang at 12:56. The bell marking the first session of the p.m. rang at 1:01. While I could probably be late without consequence for the first bell (Miss Friedstein my homeroom teacher would see to that), we were doomed if we were late for the 1:01 bell because our teacher that period was Mr. Casiano, and the class was P.E. Mr. Casiano was nicknamed Mr. Pushup because at any given moment half of his class was prone on the floor doing pushups. Hell, he'd have us do pushups as soon as look at us. Rumor had it that he'd been known to drop his own mother.

By the time we reached 79th Street, six stops from our destination, it was 12:16, and at Bay Boulevard three stops from Stillwell Avenue, it was 12:22. We were eight minutes from our fail-safe point with three stops to go. It was clear to us that we had lost all chance for a Famous. Now we were in real danger of being late, too. We had never been late for school before, so the prospect scared us.

It took eight minutes to go the final three stops. When the train pulled into the Stillwell Avenue station, we were poised at the door ready to run. When the door opened we ran to the steps, down to the street level and over to the Up staircase leading to the northbound train. Taking the stairs two at a time, we climbed to the platform, only to find that we needn't have bothered. In our haste, we had forgotten that this was the last stop; the train that was going to pull out next was the one that came in last—the train we were already on. So all we had succeeded in doing was running out of the left side doors of a train, running down the steps and over to where we could run up another set of steps, to enter the same train through the right side doors. It took us a moment to realize what we had done, but when we did we just sat there laughing and laughing. The incident cost us no time and was a good tension breaker. As we rode home, fear being replaced by some degree of equanimity, we resolved to let the chips fall where they may. The whole affair was out of our hands anyway; the train would get us home when it would.

While this is what we said to one another, underneath it all I was still pulling for an OT arrival back at school, so I periodically glanced furtively at my watch. We heard the 12:56 bell when we were about a block from the school. I felt a flush of satisfaction: despite the odds and obstacles, we were going to make it.

We didn't ride the Lunchtime Express for at least a month. Our words notwithstanding, our Coney Island close encounter had robbed us of our confidence. In fact, if you had asked me immediately after the event, I would have told you that my days of train riding were over, that discretion was the better part of valor. But eighth graders being as they are, discretion doesn't go a long way. So after about six weeks, valor renewed, we entertained again the thought of One Last Ride.

During our year of train and bus riding, we sometimes liked to have a destination. That seemed to give our meaningless escapade some credence, a flimsy rationale. Often, we would visit my aunt who lived on Avenue L, two blocks west of Coney

Island Avenue. Not only was Aunt Jean very hospitable and very nice, she was also remarkably cool for someone her age. My traveling companions seemed to appreciate her almost as much as I did, so there was never any argument about using her as our destination.

Well, after we decided to take one last ride, we had to decide on the destination. Should we try again for the Famous? Should we visit Aunt Jean? Should we try for a new distance record? In the end, it was Marty who won the day with an irrefutable argument. "Why," he said, "do we always have to go to see Jerry's aunt? Why can't we go to see my aunt?" So we went to see his aunt because, at the end of it all, let's face it, how can you argue against such logic? There was only one question I had of him. "Do you know how to get there?"

"Certainly," he shot back, insulted.

"OK, OK," I said, verbally backpedaling. "Don't get mad. It's just that we almost blew it when we went to Coney Island, and that scared me. I don't want to blow it now."

"We won't blow it. I guarantee it!" said Marty.

Fifty-two minutes later the three of us were sitting on a couple of park benches on some street somewhere in the city (to this day I honestly have no idea where we were). Myles and I were sitting side by side glaring at Marty who was sitting on the opposing bench.

"Gosh, I was sure that was the right train," Marty said sheepishly.

"Well, obviously it wasn't," responded Myles. "I have no idea where we are. I mean I've never seen this neighborhood before. I don't even know if we're still in Brooklyn."

"You mean we might not be in Brooklyn? We might be in Queens, or the Bronx?" I asked, fear mounting. I hadn't considered that possibility. "If that's the case, we're screwed."

"We're screwed anyway," said Myles, looking at his watch. "It's 12:59 right now. Unless you know of a train that will get us back in minus three minutes, we're going to be late for check-in. And even if Friedstein doesn't report us late for check-in, in three minutes we'll be late for Casiano, and you know what that means."

"Yeah, it means we're screwed," I said quietly.

"What are we going to do?" Marty whined.

"Don't whine," growled Myles. "You know I hate it when you whine."

"Well, what are we going to do?" I said, trying to exorcise all traces of whining from my voice.

"It's simple," Myles said with confidence. He was now clearly in charge. "We find out where we are, and we retrace our steps back to school."

So we descended back into the maw that was the New York subway system one more time. Two hours and thirty minutes later, we exited the station adjacent to Montauk Junior High School. It was 3:29, and the bell to end classes for the day was just ringing as we came walking through the homeroom door. Ms. Friedstein looked up with surprise as we entered.

"Where in God's name have you been?" she said without humor. "I told you boys you'd get into trouble someday running around the city. Well, now you've done it."

"But, it was my grandmother," said Marty. "She was sick. She died. We went to her funeral."

"Don't give me any of that," Ms. Friedstein snapped. "Go right down to the principal's office. You're on detention."

So there it was. The three of us found ourselves on detention for three days. Our parents were notified and had to come in for a conference with the principal. Our permanent records were annotated with a record of our actions. We never rode the Lunchtime Express again.

Brooklyn Tech

*W*hen I was in the 6th grade, I was so poor in math that I twice failed the test for entry into the special progress program.

When I was in the 7th grade, I was near the top of the math class. Somewhere between 6th and 7th grade, math started making sense to me. It just sort of clicked in. One day my math teacher, Mrs. Michaels, said to me, "Are you going to apply to go to Brooklyn Tech?"

"What's that," I asked naively.

She replied that it was a special school in downtown Brooklyn that kids who were technically on the ball went to. I thought about it for a while and decided to apply. The only problem was that I had to take a test to enter Brooklyn Tech.

Now I hate tests. I really hate them!

But this test seemed like a good idea. Or at least going to Brooklyn Tech did. You couldn't have one without the other. So I applied.

The entry exam was given at Brooklyn Tech in May of 1955. It turned out I was not alone in wanting to apply to this advanced technology school. In my class alone, there were four of us wanting to attend Tech: Marty Wassman, Gerald Weisenberg, Gary Zisk, and me. Had it not been a school exclusively for boys, there would have been more applicants.

So on one Saturday in May we all went together down to the Tech. It was just a short train ride to Carol St. and then a short walk. When we got to the school, we found more than a thousand boys milling around waiting to take the test. This was going to be more competitive than I had thought. I later found out that for every one of the 250 slots, there were five candidates. The test took about four hours. We did math problems, wrote essays, and did all sorts of IQ puzzles. When it was all over, I felt drained.

Walking back to the subway station, we discussed the test. I quickly learned that Marty thought the test was very hard. In fact, he was sure he failed it. Gary was confident to the point of arrogance. I, myself, was not sure of the result. I still remember one of the test questions. A multiple-choice question asked us to supply the definition to a word. The word in the question was "carnivore." The answer I chose was "having fun." Gary told me the right answer was "flesh eating." He had a big laugh at my unfortunate choice.

That one question set the tenor of my day. Not only did I get that question wrong, I felt that I had gotten all the questions wrong. I decided that I wouldn't be going to Brooklyn Tech.

About three weeks later, the four of us were called from class to go down to the counselor's office. We were to receive the results of the entry tests. We waited in a small room with a table and two chairs. In walked the school counselor, Mr. Templeton, and he said, "Mr. Zisk and Mr. Weisenberg please come with me." Marty and I looked at each other. I remembered he'd said he had done poorly on the test and that he wasn't going to get in. The present situation confirmed my thought that neither was I. Gary, who was so confident, had been taken off separately.

In about five minutes, Mr. Templeton returned and closed the door behind him. Standing over us, he said, "Congratulations, boys, you made it. You both will attend Brooklyn Tech in the fall."

In the fall, Marty went to Brooklyn Tech, and I did not. You see, after the summer, my parents moved the family to Valley Stream on Long Island, so Brooklyn Tech was not in the cards for me. I was disappointed, but on balance it was a good move for me. I liked the fresh newness of Valley Stream and my new high school. I liked not being bullied at noon time. I liked the boys, and I really liked the girls! It was like discovering civilization after having been in the wilderness. It was a good move, in spite of not going to Brooklyn Tech.

Peppy le Bleu

$\mathcal{H}$e was a blue budgie—a birthday present from my parents to my sister on her 10th birthday. At first, I didn't care much for the bird. He was cute enough, but he seemed rather stupid. Little by little, however, I warmed to him. We spent more and more time together. Eventually, the bird became mine by default. Pretty soon he was my dearest friend. He sat on my glasses or on my desk while I did my homework. He sat beside me while I ate my lunch. With practice, I learned how to draw a pencil sketch of him. The blue and white puffball was drawn and redrawn and Peppy started appearing all over the house.

We quickly learned that Peppy had one cat-like characteristic: he had multiple lives. One day, I tried to catch him in mid-flight as he flew by my head. As my arm shot out, he changed direction of flight and slammed into the door jamb. As I watched with horror, Peppy fell to the floor in a limp heap. I was positive he was dead. I let out a scream, and my parents came running from the living room. My father scooped up the small, blue body and walked rapidly into the kitchen. He opened the high cabinet that served as a repository for his liquor and withdrew a bottle of scotch. He poured a small amount into a teaspoon and dunked Peppy's head into the spoon. After a moment, the bird stirred, got to his feet and walked unsteadily toward his cage. The next day he seemed quite normal, although it did seem that from then on he did hang out around the liquor cabinet.

Our family dog was a collie named Robin. Robin and Peppy had a mutual understanding: They ignored one another. I never saw Robin show any interest whatsoever in the bird. One afternoon while Robin slept on the threshold between my bedroom and the hallway, Peppy was out of his cage and sitting on my glasses. Without warning, he decided to go back to his cage, which was in the next room. As he flew low through the open doorway, he startled Robin, who reacted by snapping at the projectile. The dog's aim was good. His jaws came down on Peppy's tail feathers and separated them from his body.

Relieved of his feathers, Peppy fell to the floor. I ran over and picked him up. The place where the feathers had been attached was bloody. Had the dog been a few microseconds quicker, he would have bitten the bird in half. Robin, feathers in mouth, looked on as I carried the bird to his cage and gently placed him inside. My mother dabbed peroxide on Peppy's wound. Within several weeks Peppy had reacquired his tail feathers. From that point on, he carefully watched his altitude when flying over Robin.

August 15, 1954, was a landmark day in the life of my family. It was the day that we moved from Brooklyn to Long Island. It was also the day of Peppy's greatest adventure.

To assist in the move, my parents had hired a moving company. While the men were moving the furniture into the van, I was in my room playing with Peppy. Unknown to me, the movers had opened all of the outside doors to expedite the job. When I opened the door of my bedroom, Peppy flew out of the room towards his cage. Only now there was bright light streaming through an open door. Attracted by the light, Peppy flew through the door and out into the Brooklyn air. It all happened in a heartbeat.

Frantically I raced outside and scanned the sky. There was nothing in sight. Peppy was gone.

I was distraught. My parents tried to console me. They told me it was just a bird and that I could get another. Of course this did no good at all. Peppy was not "just a bird." He was my friend, and I had just lost him forever. I cried and cried. I asked my parents if we could stay in the house longer to give Peppy a chance to return. Unfortunately we could not. We were to leave the next morning and nothing, especially a five-dollar parakeet, would change that.

I spent a sleepless night replaying the incident, changing the ending in my imagination. But when morning came, Peppy was still gone.

As I sat silently at the breakfast table, knowing that I would be leaving in an hour, my morale hit rock bottom. I was so low that I did not hear the phone ring. My father answered it, but I did not hear the conversation until he mentioned Peppy's name. At once I perked up and started listening. The person on the other end of the line spoke into the phone as though it were a megaphone, so I could hear both sides of the conversation.

"Are you the people who lost the bird yesterday?" the voice said.

"Yes," my father replied.

"Well," the voice continued, "last night, Bob and Sally Denish came to dinner at our house."

"They are our next door neighbors," my father interjected.

"Yes, I know," the voice said. "They told us of your missing bird. We were having dessert while talking about the incident when we heard a tapping at the window. There, standing on the outside sill was a blue parakeet. We opened the window, and it hopped in. I think we have your bird."

I couldn't believe my ears. Was it possible? Had a miracle occurred? Had God heard my prayers?

In a flash I was on my bike, transport cage in hand. Peppy's savior lived only five blocks away. In three minutes I was at the door ringing the bell. The door opened, and a man let me in and led me to a back bedroom. There in the room standing on a desk was Peppy. I cannot remember, either before or since, feeling such unbounded joy.

The rest of the move went off without a hitch. In two weeks I started ninth grade at South High School in Valley Stream, Long Island. During the next four years, as my mind turned to other things, Peppy became less important to me. As Puff learned from Jackie, little boys don't live forever. In 1959 I went off to college. Sometime during the second semester of that school year, my parents informed me on the phone that Peppy had died. I nodded, hung up the phone, went back to my dorm room, and continued to do the physics problem I was working on.

The Fight

*F*or most of my youth, from the age of one through the age of fourteen, I lived in the house my grandparents owned in Brooklyn, on 183 East 5th Street, between Fort Hamilton Parkway and Caton Avenue. On the corner of 5th and Caton was the home of our next-door neighbors, the Litvins, Hilda and Mitch Litvin and their daughter Judy.

The Litvins had been our neighbors for as long as I could remember. One year older than I, Judy was, with the exception of Albey Reiner, my best friend and teacher. As our parents were good friends, we played together every day. She always had a new game to teach. It was Judy who taught me Ringalevio, Blind Man's Bluff, and, when we were old enough to play in the street, my all-time favorite, Johnny, May I Cross Your River. Moreover, being female, Judy could provide instruction that Albey could not provide. I was five years old when she introduced me to a new game. We were playing in my backyard when she led me, surreptitiously, to a place where an old oak tree blocked our view of the house. "Do you want to play Doctor?" she asked.

"What's that?" I asked naively.

"It goes like this. First I take my clothes off and you examine me. Then you take your clothes off and I examine you. It's fun!"

"I don't know," I said dubiously.

"I'll go first," she said, unbuttoning her shirt. Judy was unstoppable once she had her mind set on something. She was a force in my life as powerful as my parents. I had long before learned not to argue with her, especially when it came to deciding which game to play.

At first, the game seemed very strange, but after a while I got into it. In the end, I found the experience most interesting, and it reinforced my faith in Judy as a teacher. Something told me, however, not to mention the incident to my parents. I didn't, but they figured it out. Possibly, it was the fact that when I returned home, my polo shirt was on backward and my pants were inside out. Possibly they were aided by the fact that, when pressed by my mother, I admitted the whole thing—right down to the last detail. And their response? Well, it was rather mild—not at all corporal. They just said that it was probably a good idea if we didn't do that anymore. Usually, I obeyed my parents to the best of my ability, but in this case there were powerful forces working in opposition to my parents' admonition. During the next few years we played Doctor several times, and it was no longer necessary for Judy to urge me forward.

While I went to the public school, P.S. 130, on the corner of East 5th Street and Fort Hamilton Parkway, Judy went to a private school, which, I believed, gave her a superior slant. She was always coming up with concepts I had never heard of, like the time she told me she was going to her Ami. This annoyed me because I felt that if Judy had an Ami, I should have one too. So, I went to my mother and asked her where my Ami was. She smiled at me and explained that my Ami was really a city called Miami and that the Litvins had a second home in that city. I did not realize it at the moment, but that city was soon to claim Judy and end our friendship.

One morning, while I was playing on the front porch, a big moving van pulled up in front of the Litvin's house. By the end of the day, they were gone. They had moved to their other home in Miami, and I never saw any of them again.

In time, a new family, the Thomases, moved in next door. The parents were older than my parents, and they had three children—all boys. The boys were in their twenties, married, and lived with their parents. Altogether there were eight people living next door. Since there was no one my age, I paid little attention to them. My parents told me that they were contractors (whatever that meant). I had no idea that inside that house a force was growing, a force that would catapult me into the next chapter of my life.

In early 1954, my father noticed that the sidewalk in front of our house was badly cracked. He discussed the problem with my mother, and they decided to ask the Thomases to do the job. They accepted, and the next Saturday they started the task. First, they used two-by-fours to build the forms for the three slabs of cement that were to be constructed. Then, they poured bags of concrete into a wheelbarrow, added water, and mixed the cement. Finally, they poured the cement into the forms, and smoothed the thick, gray liquid with a trowel. All of this occurred under the watchful gaze of my father.

"Well," my father said to me, "all they have to do now is wait for the cement to dry, remove the forms, and they are through."

"How long should that take?" I asked.

"Oh, tomorrow or the next day," said the elder Thomas.

Two days later, the youngest Thomas boy was sent over to remove the forms. I watched as he pried off the two-by-fours that formed the perimeter of the job. They easily gave way before his crowbar. But when he tried to remove the two pieces of wood that separated the three slabs, they would not budge. The separator strips were locked in tight. He pulled, pried, and smashed, but the wood would not move.

"If I hit it any harder," he said over his shoulder to me, "I'm afraid I'll break the cement. I'd better go tell them." And off he went into the house. A few moments later Thomas, Sr. came out the front door trailed by his three sons and one of his daughters-in-law. He walked up to the job, kneeled down, and looked intently at the juncture of the first two slabs. He frowned and muttered to himself, "These two should have been removed yesterday. Now they're stuck."

Just at this point my father came out of the house. He walked up to us and said, "What's going on?"

"The slabs are done," Thomas, Sr., said to my father.

Quizzically my father first looked at the slabs and then at the speaker. "What about those two strips between the slabs?" he asked.

"Oh, they are OK there," said Thomas.

"No, they are not!" retorted my father. "There are supposed to be spaces between the slabs for expansion. Those strips are filling the expansion space. If the strips are left in, the slabs will crack in the summer."

"It's too late to get the strips out!" growled Thomas.

"Well, it's a botched job then," my father shot back.

"It's good enough!" Thomas shouted.

"I am not paying for a botched job!" yelled my father.

"It's good enough," repeated Thomas.

"Go to hell!" my father screamed, and turned on his heels and walked away.

Well, Mr. Thomas refused to remove the pieces of wood between the slabs, and my father refused to pay him. Neither family spoke to any member of the other family.

The stalemate remained until Sunday, July 18, 1954, a day that had the makings of greatness—possibly one of the best days of my life. It was, you see, the day after my Bar Mitzvah, the ancient rite of passage for thirteen year-old Jewish boys. On the previous day, which was the Sabbath, I had to demonstrate my manhood by leading a hunting party into uncharted lands, killing a woolly mammoth with only a spear, and strangling a 500-pound wild boar with my bare hands. Of course, since none of these things was possible in Brooklyn, the Lords of Tradition came up with an equally hideous way to torture young teenage males. They deprive them of their playtime for four years and make them sit in regimented rows learning to recite some meaningless (to them) words in a foreign language that seemingly no one understands so that they might on some Sabbath near their thirteenth birthday make a fool of themselves in front of their family and friends and a host of strangers by reciting those same words while standing exposed and vulnerable on the raised temple altar.

I hated every aspect of the preparation for my Bar Mitzvah, and I dreaded the day itself. But now that it was over, my life could start again. I could once again appreciate the good things around me: the blue sky, the freedom of summer, French fries from Nathan's, and the Giants' slim lead in the National League.

I awoke that Sunday morning with an ineffable feeling of well-being. It was going to be a beautiful day—somewhere in the 70s. I called my friend Myles on the phone and invited him to come over to play ball. Usually, because he lived much closer to me, I would have called Albey to play ball, but he was away for the summer.

Myles said that he had some chores to do and could come at noon. While I waited for him, I looked at the gifts that I had received the day before. Most of them were cash or bonds—about $175 worth—but I also received a dictionary, a thesaurus, a small telescope, and two wristwatches. One of the watches was of the Mickey Mouse variety; the other was a rather formal-looking Benrus. Lastly, I looked at the gold ring that my grandfather had given me. The band contained two snakes reminiscent of a caduceus and the initials "AEW," and it was studded with a relatively large diamond. I was holding the ring in my hand when Myles walked into my bedroom.

"I'm here," he redundantly announced. "Let's go!"

"Do you want to walk over to the parade grounds? We can use a hardball."

"Naw," he said. "I gotta go home soon. Let's use a Spauldeen and play in front of the house."

"OK," I said as I grabbed the pink rubber ball that was sitting on my desk. "Let's go!" We ran outside and started throwing the Spauldeen back and forth. As usual, as we continued play, we increased the distance between us. Then we started throwing the ball in long high arcs, mimicking to the best of our young ability Major League pop-ups and flies. Farther and farther, higher and higher flew the pink spheroid. And, as always happens, one throw went slightly awry.

As the ball left my hand, I could tell that it was ever so slightly off the mark. By the time it reached the top of its arc, I knew, as did Myles, that it was going to come down very near a parked car we had been carefully avoiding. I was not worried, given that the soft pink rubber was quite forgiving. Myles knew this also, but there was another issue at play: pride. The pride of giving every chance your all. The pride when one makes a great or near-great catch. The pride of thwarting the collision of ball and glass.

So, even though there was no real danger to the car, Myles went for the ball. Moving sideways, trying to get under the falling Spauldeen, he put out his arm, horizontally, feeling for obstacles. Closer and closer he got to the car. Soon he was bending backward over the hood, reaching and straining to get his hand under the descending projectile, which was now no more than ten to fifteen feet in the air. It looked to me as though he was going to catch it. I could not have imagined that the success or failure of that catch would be the factor that would determine the future course of my life.

At the last millisecond, a slight gust of wind altered the flight of the relatively low-mass ball. It flew past his outstretched hand and caromed off the passenger's-side windshield wiper. It bounced high in the air, leaving the scene of the collision at a random angle, flew over the Thomases' fence and came to rest squarely in the middle of their backyard.

In normal times I would have hopped the fence, retrieved the ball and been out of there before anybody knew what happened. But those were not normal times. The tension between the two families was palpable, and it froze me in my tracks. I had a strong feeling that it would not be so easy to get my ball back—especially since Mr. Thomas, who had been sitting on his porch, was now striding purposefully toward the small pink sphere.

I stood there, speechless, gazing at Mr. Thomas, who was now gazing back at me, equally mute, while he tossed the ball, George Raft-like, over and over again, about a foot into the air and let it drop into his huge hand.

Then, without a word, he spun on his heels and started walking back toward his house, the pink hostage still in hand.

"Give the kid back his ball!" came the sharp command from the porch of my house.

I spun and looked up onto the porch. I had not realized until that moment that some of my family was watching the progress of my catch with Myles. There was my father, who, after he shouted the last command, had risen to his feet and started approaching the stairs that led down to the very same concrete slabs, still harboring the wooden spacers that started the whole sorry business. Also there, still seated, were my mother and paternal grandmother, who was visiting for the afternoon.

"I'll give the ball back when you pay me what you owe me," said Thomas, his voice rising.

"I'll pay you what I owe you when you do the job right," countered my father, angrily. Now he was walking slowly down the porch steps.

"The job was done right!" yelled Thomas, walking toward my father.

"It was a botched job!" screamed my father, slightly quickening his pace toward Thomas.

"You dirty kike. You Jew bastard . . ." Thomas started.

He never got to finish his sentence, for when he uttered the word "kike," my father broke into a sprint. Seeing him approach, Thomas responded in kind. They met in the middle swinging at one another. Neither landed a punch. Out of the corner of my eye, I saw the three Thomas sons racing from their porch followed by one of their wives. They were on my father in a flash and down he went. The four Thomas men, now totally in control, started kicking at my father and shouting curse words.

All of a sudden a new person entered the frame—my Grandmother who had been watching from the porch. When she saw her son being attacked by four men, she came racing to his aid. The Thomas wife intercepted her, threw her to the ground and started kicking her.

I stood frozen in horror. I said nothing. I did nothing. I just stood there. Fortunately, Myles had the presence of mind to run for help. He raced the hundred yards between our house and 193 East 5th Street, the home of Bob Leslie, a good family friend and an officer of the New York City Police. In under a minute Bob arrived and quickly ended the battle. But that minute took its toll. Both my father and grandmother were badly bruised from the kicks and blows, and each had suffered cuts and contusions. The Thomases were, however, totally untouched. My father and grandmother were taken into the house to clean up. My father's most serious injury was a cut over his left eyebrow. My grandmother was more angry than hurt. She was seething, her hair was disheveled, and she sat in the living room shaking her fist in the direction she believed the Thomas house lay.

My father, too, was beside himself with anger. He yelled, "I'm going to sue the bastards! I'm going to take them for everything they have! I'm going to show them that they can't get away with pushing me around!" And so it came to pass that my father filed a lawsuit against the Thomases for assault, while they filed a counter suit for failure to pay a debt.

As the court date approached, I became more and more afraid of the meeting in the courtroom or, possibly, outside the courtroom. I was afraid that there might be another fight, only this time Bob Leslie would not be there. I was afraid for my father's safety. I became so nervous that my parents decided that I would not go to the courtroom but, rather, would stay home with my grandparents. So I did not see the court proceedings. What I was told was that the judge admonished both parties for being neighbors who were failing to get along. Then he threw both cases out and told them to settle their differences like civilized people. But that didn't happen. Instead, the shunning and the silence between the families continued.

At this point in the story I had to think of a way to end it. I had originally intended the story to be about the fight and so, in fact, it was. But is that all? Was there nothing else here? Then I thought of changing the title to "The Worst Day in My Life," or something like that. But was it really the worst day of my life? I had seen my first physical violence face to face, but is that the only way of looking at it? Louise Hay, in her book You Can Heal Your Life *says that we create our own reality. The spins given to the "facts" during recent presidential elections gives ample evidence for the validity of this concept. So, was there a way to spin the outcome of the whole affair? After all, if the universe is, as Einstein suggests, relative, then the interpretation of events is nothing but perception.*

And indeed there was a way to spin the affair. It was a good spin—a very good spin. Usually a spin of 90 degrees or more is considered adequate. This spin was 172.5 degrees! That's almost a perfect spin. How can one spin this story? Listen!

After the court battle, the tension became worse than ever. I was afraid to walk past their house. Something had to give. Finally, my parents hit upon a solution: we would move!

I was in torment. On one side, we were going to get away from the Thomases. That was great. But on the other hand, I was going to be leaving my friends. In my memory, I had never moved before.

Before I knew it, we were house hunting. My parents decided that we would move to Long Island, and we looked in each town. After a few months, we found a new development that we could afford in the town of Valley Stream. The development, if you can believe it, was called Green Acres, even though no one owned as much as an acre and there was no tree higher than three feet in sight. They started building our house in the fall of 1954. It was finished in August 1955, and we moved on September 2nd. When I went to register for 9th grade, I found that they had just completed construction of a new high school, Valley Stream South High School. I was to be a member of the second graduating class, the class of '59. And as far as being a new student, well, all the students in the area were new. Everyone was looking for, and open to, new friendships.

I thrived in the suburban environment. I loved my new home, community, and, above all, my school. I became lighting director for our class plays, treasurer of the student council, business manager of the class yearbook, and vice-president of the senior class. I grew socially as never before, in part because of the opportunities that presented themselves in this fecund environment.

Most importantly, in my freshman year, I met my wife-to-be, Broni. For three years, we were just good friends. During that time she was dating a guy from our rival North High School, while I went through about a girl per year. When we found ourselves free at the same time in November of 1958, we started dating.

While my parents wanted me to go to college in New York City, Broni encouraged me to go to an out-of-town school. Broni won. In the fall of 1959, I enrolled at Worcester Polytechnic Institute, in Massachusetts. It was a difficult four years, but in June of 1963, I graduated with a Baccalaureate in Physics.

At this point, I was offered a job in New York City with the New York Telephone Company. Broni, however, thought that I should accept an offer to go to graduate school in Astronomy at UCLA. So after we were married in the summer of 1963, off we went to LA, ostensibly for a two-year Master's program. But the West was so beautiful and free, we knew that we could never go back to the East Coast.

While in the Master's program at UCLA, I accepted a job teaching a night Astronomy course at Santa Monica College, a local two-year school. I enjoyed teaching so much that when, in 1969, a full-time job for an Astronomer opened up at SMC, I applied for it and was given the position. However, by 1976, the air pollution in LA had become unbearable, so when a position in Astronomy opened at Santa Rosa Junior College, I gladly headed north.

In 1987, after a three-year illness, Broni died of breast cancer, and in 1990, I married Pam, the daughter of our department secretary. I taught at SRJC a total of 27 years, until my retirement in May of 2003. In 2000, we moved to The Sea Ranch on the Northern California Coast. It is, in my opinion, the most beautiful place on Earth.

As I look back on my life and the decisions that I made, I would not change a thing. The place I live, my educational choices, my profession, the women in my life, all these have all been perfect—just what I needed at the time. But none of these things probably would have happened if it were not for The Fight. In the end I'd have to say that August 12, 1954, was the best day of my life, in fact made my life. And I have Myles to thank for it. If he had caught that ball, I almost certainly would not be here today. I would probably still be living in Brooklyn.

Fallen Angel

*W*e moved into our new home on August 15, 1955. I was fourteen years old. It did not matter to me that our house was in a new tract called Green Acres where nothing was green and no one had as much as one acre of land. I was finished with Brooklyn and Brooklyn was finished with me. Gone were the Gremlins. Gone was Willie Trumbull. Gone was Montauk Junior High School. I was finally home!

But there was a problem, or at least so my parents thought. I was the new kid on the block, so I didn't have any friends. Accordingly, my mother set out to remedy the situation. She called around and found out that there was going to be a meeting of the Green Acres Youth Group on Friday night. I didn't really want to go, but my mother, playing the guilt/ trump card with exceptional skill, appealed to my sensibilities as a good son and, in the end, I went.

When I arrived at the youth group meeting Friday night, I found myself in a barn-like structure within which had gathered about forty boys and girls, equally divided, and roughly my age. The program for the evening consisted of about a dozen exercises or games designed, as they said, to break the ice. The only one of these games that I remember, and the highlight of the evening for me, was the game of Musical Boys. The game was played like Musical Chairs, except that on each chair in the line there sat a boy. From that point on, it was business as usual.

We started with approximately twenty boys sitting on twenty chairs, all in a straight line. The girls walked in an oval orbit around the boys while someone played a song on an old stereo. The organizers made sure that there was one less boy than there were girls at all times during the game. When the music stopped, girls all ran for the nearest boy and threw themselves on his lap. Because there was one more girl than there were boys, one girl would be left standing. This girl was out of the game. The organizers would then reduce the number of boys in the line by one and start the music again. Then the girls would start walking around the line of boys until the music stopped and again would come the mad scramble.

The point of the whole thing was that when a girl sat on a boy's lap they would introduce themselves. In this way, the adults who organized the event reasoned, the girls and boys would become familiar with one another.

I'm positive that the organizers were sincere in their hopes that this game would be a good icebreaker. However, having taken part in the game, I am just as confident that no one on the organization committee was a physicist. If there had been a physicist in the group, he or she would have known the difference between mass and momentum and would have realized that the energy imparted to a stationary target (boy) by a speeding projectile (girl) increases as the square of the velocity of the projectile. Alas, no one took this physical law into account, so the boys on the chairs became targets and the girls became battering rams. Every time the music stopped, I closed my eyes and steeled myself for the soon-to-come impact. Praying for the contest to end, I kept my eyes closed, even during the playing of the music. I no longer could bear seeing the impending collision.

For ten or twelve rounds, the music played, accompanied by the sound of feet scraping the floor, and when the music stopped, I braced myself for another collision. But this time it did not come. Instead there settled on me a weight so slight I was not sure that it was really there. I opened my eyes to see what leaf had fallen on me, and when I did I found myself looking into eyes bluer than I thought possible. I expanded my field of view—zooming out as it were—to encompass the entire visage. Nothing was lost or diminished. The face surrounding those eyes was, if it were possible, more beautiful than the eyes. And the complexion, ditto. And the hair, ditto. And the smile . . . well, the smile was the stuff of dreams—the reason wars are fought.

"Hi!" she said, eyes large and bright. "I'm Susan."

I was transfixed. I couldn't move. I was mesmerized, paralyzed, and hypnotized. Seconds went by. How many, I cannot guess. I must have appeared retarded.

"The word you're searching for is 'hello,'" she added, playfully.

As I opened my mouth to say something, anything, the music started again. Before I could utter a word, she slowly and silently gravitated upward and away to join the throng of girls orbiting the line of chair-boys, which was now ten strong.

I was distraught. She was the most exquisite creature I had ever seen and, when my moment came, I blew it. I felt like crawling into a hole and pulling it in after me. So preoccupied with self-pity was I that I failed to hear the music stop once again. Once again the scramble of footsteps and then . . . once again the leaf settled on my knee. I raised my gaze from the floor and met hers. Her eyes were still smiling. What should I say to her?

"Don't you have a name?" she asked.

"I'm Jerry."

"Hello, Jerry. Nice to meet you."

Once again the music started and once again she was gone: "Back soon. Don't get lost."

And she was. And again. And again. It was amazing. She had obviously found some pattern in the timing of the music and synchronized her gait to that pattern, for almost every time the music stopped, she was within a few feet of me. In this way, our mini-rendezvous continued until, finally, it was my turn to leave the lineup.

Very soon after that our parents came to fetch us, so I did not have the opportunity (even if I could have found the nerve) to talk to her again that night.

In the days that followed, I made inquiries about her of my new friend Mike Kerr and discovered the details. Her name was Susan Jonas, and she lived on Eastwood Lane, next door to Mike, and three or four blocks from my house. She had a younger brother and a dog. And then, the fatal flaw—the death knell. She was going into the 8th grade. I was going into the 9th grade.

Why fatal? Because where I came from (Brooklyn), it was customary to date people only from your own grade. To do otherwise would be to invite abuse. I was stuck. I liked her a lot, but I was new in the area and I did not want to commit a social faux pas. So I did not follow up on our initial encounter. She must have been hurt because she had let me know by her actions that she liked me, but she got nothing in return.

The days turned into months and the months into years. We saw each other, in passing, every day and whenever we did, her eyes would brighten as I am sure did mine. Whenever we had the opportunity, we would spar with one another good-naturedly—an obvious mutual flirtation. If I would pass her in the hall between classes and not acknowledge her—even if I didn't see her—she would stop me and say, "The word you are searching for is 'hello,'" or, "The words you are searching for are 'good morning,'" or some variation on that theme.

But beyond that—nothing. My relationships came and went, lasting from a few months to a year, all with girls from my own age group.

Finally, in the last month of my senior year, Susan acted unilaterally. She asked me out on a date. We went to a party at one of her friend's homes and then, although it was several miles, we walked home. The evening was a magical experience. We joked around, had serious moments, and spent times in mutual silence. It was as though we had, at the same time, been together for a millennium and met just five minutes before.

And in the days following the date I did—nothing. I was still hamstrung by the same stupid code. In the fall, I went off to college, and when I graduated, I married a girl I had known in high school. She was my age.

In 1974, about fifteen years after I left high school, I had occasion to run into my old high school buddy Mike Kerr. At some point in the conversation I asked him if he knew anything about his next-door neighbor, Susan. He said, yes, his parents had kept in touch with hers. Susan, he said sadly, had died during childbirth just two years earlier. She was just thirty years old.

Many times, I've had to choke back tears when I think of her. I feel sad not only for her, but for me as well. Sad for the lost opportunity, for the fulfillment that never was. And although I know it's not rational, I feel guilt for forcing her along a world line that ended in her premature death. I just know that it wasn't supposed to be that way. It smacks of hubris, but I have this feeling that I upset the natural order of things when I rejected her for what really amounted to a nothing, a silly adolescent code of . . .

The lovely girl I thought was an angel has fallen, and the word I am searching for is "forever."

69

*M*y life was over . . . toast. I'd be thrown out of school . . . no more career. My girlfriend would never talk to me again . . . . Neither would my parents. I had never been so scared before in my life.

I looked to my right for an avenue of escape. The door handle and window handle had been removed. I glanced over to the left . . . same thing. In front of me, dimly silhouetted by the headlamps, was a criss-cross iron grate that served as a barrier to freedom. Even if the grate had not been there, there was no freedom in that direction. In the front seat, similarly silhouetted, were the outlines of the two Connecticut highway patrolmen who, minutes before, had placed me under arrest on suspicion of grand theft and pushed me roughly into the back seat of the patrol car.

The car glided slowly down the empty highway in the pre-dawn hours of the Connecticut night. At the wheel, Officer Frank Householder, the officer who had formally arrested me, gazed intently at the roadsides, first to the right, then to the left. To his right, the second officer—I never did get his name—played the patrol car's powerful searchlight along the roadside.

"Where are they?" Householder demanded, turning his head slightly to the right. "Up ahead . . . on the right . . .

next to that route sign in that gully," I replied in a hoarse whisper. The car rolled to a stop at the place indicated. The two officers moved in unison. As Householder reached for the radio's microphone, his partner snapped the shotgun out of its holder under the dashboard. He rolled down the window and leveled the shotgun at the gully. Householder's booming voice, amplified by the patrol car's PA system, split the night.

THIS IS THE POLICE! WE KNOW YOU'RE THERE. WE HAVE YOUR FRIENDS. COME ON OUT AND KEEP YOUR HANDS WHERE WE CAN SEE THEM.

Within two seconds, there was a response. Two heads popped over the lip of the gully, followed immediately by two torsos and four scrambling feet. Hands high over their heads, Steve and Lee walked into the headlamp beams of the patrol car. Seemingly out of nowhere, a second patrol car pulled up. Almost before it stopped, a policeman jumped out of the passenger side and swept Steve and Lee into the back seat. As rapidly as it appeared, the car sped away into the blackness. Householder, who was still behind the wheel, turned to me.

"All right," he said, "Let's take care of you."

Six months to the day earlier, I had started my college education at Worcester Polytechnic Institute in Worcester, Massachusetts. Nowadays, it is a big coeducational university, but in those days it was a smallish school (fewer than 900 students) and not a female in sight. Perhaps because of the social vacuum, fraternities were prominent at WPI. Ninety percent of the student body belonged to them.

When the time for pledging arrived, I decided to join Alpha Epsilon Pi fraternity. I really had little choice in the matter, as it was the only house that would have me. You see, at Tech in those years, AEPi was the only Jewish fraternity. The other nine houses, in an apparent gesture of friendship, eschewed pledging Jewish freshmen in order to assure that the "APES" would secure their quota of pledges.

I hated being a pledge. It was demeaning and insulting. We were as slaves, taking orders from all who wished to give them. At one point, about two months into our pledgeship, the whole pledge class was summarily called to the fraternity house. There in the living room was the assembled brotherhood—65 strong. We were informed that it was time for the annual treasure hunt. The treasure hunt consisted of a list of ten items, each of which, theoretically, could be readily found in the home, or at least in town. The pledge class was to round up these objects. Even today, I can still recall most of the list:

1. Autographed photo of Bob Cousy
2. Hood ornament from 1960 Mercedes Benz 350 SEL
3. Auto license plate from the state of Alaska
4. "Institute Rd" street sign
5. Framed Elaine Stewart centerfold

The rest of the items did not matter. It was #4 that started the ball rolling. It was #4 that would ultimately lead to my undoing.

That same night, the thirteen in our pledge class had a meeting concerning the treasure hunt. We decided to order the ten-item list by ease of acquisition. After the reordering, the Institute Rd. street sign was second (just after the centerfold). We also divvied up the list, each taking one or two items. I ended up with the street sign and some innocuous second item. Strangely, the road sign generated much interest, so when it was all over there were no less than four of us on the Road Sign Liberation Committee, or RSLC, as we called ourselves.

The next night the RSLC had its first meeting. We decided when to carry out the caper, who would bring the tools and who would hide the booty once it was liberated. Since two of us on the committee were roommates, we determined that it was safest if Bob and I kept the sign in our dorm room. Both Steve and Lee had roommates who were pledging other fraternities, so it would present a security problem to use either of their rooms.

When the appointed time arrived, the project went off without a hitch. One night at about 3:00 a.m. we all met outside our dorm. Within twenty minutes we were back, me carrying the tools and Bob carrying the liberated sign.

At first we kept it carefully hidden, but soon news of its existence spread around the dorm. Within a week, so many people were stopping by to see it that it was "out" more than it was "in." Finally, we just propped it on the bureau.

When our pledge class acquired all the items on the list, we brought them to the fraternity house. Even though the project had been completed successfully, a problem remained. My bureau top was vacant . . . and so was our room. With the artifact gone, our popularity waned. We felt abandoned, but now that we were pros we knew what we could do about it. We could get another sign. At the same time, both Lee and Steve decided the same thing. They each wanted signs for their rooms. The game was afoot.

The fad started as quickly as the turn of the tides. One moment road signs were for roads—the next they were for hanging in dorm rooms. Hardly a room in the place was without one. A quasi-culture grew up around the larceny. We, after all, had our values. No signs were to be taken that would put anyone in jeopardy. This meant no stop signs, speed limit signs or road configuration signs (such as signs warning about curves). We mostly limited ourselves to signs that gave the names of places—this or that road or street.

But, things being as they are, it started to escalate. Soon we noticed that the signs being "liberated" were getting larger and larger. People were also going farther and farther to get their signs. Having been, we thought, the initiators of the process, the four of us felt some duty to stay on top, or at least in the running. One night we were in Bob's 1959 VW Beetle on our way to Boston. Boston is about forty miles from Worcester, and we went often, mostly to go to a movie or, as on this night, to see the Sox at Fenway. Anyway, as we entered the Mass Pike at the Auburn entrance, we passed under a rather largish green and white sign that said simply "Massachusetts Turnpike." It was high over our heads, so we really couldn't tell how big it was. It was clear, however, that it was of record size. We quickly decided to take a shot at it—only, of course, at another, less crowded time.

That same night, after the ballgame and a couple of hours at some Newbury Street ice cream parlor, we exited the pike at the Auburn exit. It was after 2:00 a.m. We parked the car about 100 yards past the tollbooth and walked over to the onramp to the eastbound lanes. Soon we were standing under the sign. Bob looked dubious.

"Are you sure it's not too big?" he asked hesitantly.

"Don't be silly," I replied. "Big is what we're after."

"I don't know," said Steve. "How're we gonna get it down?"

"Easy," I said. "I'll climb up on the side and walk out on that overhang until I get to the sign."

The sign was attached to a large metal structure that spanned the roadway. On each side of the roadway was a vertical metal tower about thirty feet high. Connecting the two towers was a horizontal metal span about fifty feet long. The sign was attached to the horizontal span.

"That looks dangerous," Lee said.

"No problem," I called back over my shoulder as I walked toward the closer of the two vertical members. I remember thinking "piece of cake" as I stood at the base of the tower looking up.

Climbing had always been my strong suit. As a child, whenever my mother would go outside looking for me, she would generally find me on top of something—a neighboring roof, the billboard in the vacant lot, a tree. She didn't know where it would be. She only knew that it would be up.

Standing next to the vertical sign support, I sized up the project. I would need two wrenches, both adjustable, and two lengths of rope, each about thirty feet long. These items, and more, we carried in the back of the VW. We were always ready for action. I got the tools of liberation from the car, stuffed them into an old daypack, slung it over my shoulder, and proceeded to climb the vertical sign support.

"Piece of cake" was an understatement—the structure was apparently designed for climbing. There were handholds and footholds all over it. I quickly ascended the thirty feet to the horizontal part, where the ease-of-access continued. Running along the entire length of the horizontal archway was a narrow, flat walkway about 1½ feet wide. This was too easy!

I walked quickly out to the left edge of the sign. It was held onto its support by two one-inch bolts. The sign must have been newly installed because there was no trace of rust on the bolts. Using the two wrenches, I quickly removed the upper left-hand bolt. Because of the other three bolts, of course, the sign did not budge. Before doing anything else,

I slipped the rope through the hole vacated by the bolt and tied the upper left-hand corner of the sign tight to its support. Next, I removed the lower left-hand bolt and tossed it into my daypack along with the first bolt. I then sidestepped over to the right side of the sign. This was actually the most difficult part of the operation because I was in front of the sign at this point, so my access to the handholds on the horizontal support was blocked.

Once at the right side of the sign, I removed the upper-right bolt and, as on the left side, used the second length of rope to tie the sign to its support. Finally, I removed the lower-right bolt. Now the sign was supported only by the two pieces of rope through the top holes.

Carefully bracing myself, I untied the rope that held the sign against the right-hand support. When it came loose, I became the support for half the sign. "Christ," I gasped. The damn thing was almost as heavy as I was. If I had not braced myself before untying that knot, that sign would have pulled me over the edge of the walkway, and I would have fallen the thirty feet to the ground.

"Shit!" I yelled down to my friends below, "they must've made this goddam thing out of Osmium. Be careful when it comes down—it's HEAVY!"

Slowly, I lowered the right side of the sign, the left side, pivoting about the left-hand rope as an axis, remaining at fixed.

After about a minute, the sign was hanging vertically, the left side still tied to its support, the right side hanging freely, some four to six feet off the ground. The last phase was easy. With Bob, Steve, and Lee taking the weight off the final support rope by lifting up on the sign, I untied the rope and lowered the sign to the ground. *Quelle Victoire!*

As I made my way back to the left-hand vertical support, the rest of the team carried the sign over to the car. It was all over but the shouting! We were back! Kings of the hill!

I quickly descended the support tower, ran over to the car, and pulled up short. Something was wrong. Standing motionless next to the car, holding up the sign, was the team. None of them said a word; they just looked at me. I looked back at them.

"What's wrong?" I asked. They said nothing as their eyes traveled to the sign.

And then I saw it . . . or rather, didn't see it. The car was gone. Well, not really gone as much as hidden. To free their hands to open the doors, Bob, Steve and Lee had leaned the sign up against the car. From where I stood, about thirty feet from the car, our folly was apparent. What the rest of the team had suspected, but I had denied, was clearly true. The sign stood at least one foot higher and five feet longer than the VW in which we proposed to take the damn thing home.

We looked at one another for a long moment before Bob started laughing. Before another ten seconds elapsed, we were all on the ground, holding our sides, laughing out of control, tears streaming down our faces.

Not knowing what else to do, we carried the sign to the roadside, propped it up and left it there. In fifteen minutes we were back at the dorm and in our rooms.

We never told anyone about our misdeed. It was worse than dropping a foul pop in the stands at Fenway. After all, we were physicists and engineers. We were going to build skyscrapers and bridges and design rockets that would fly to the moon. It would not do to let it be known that we had thought we could put a 6' x 20' sign in a 5' x 15' car.

The incident was depressing. We had failed to deliver the mail . . . to bring home the bacon. We had to make amends, to elevate ourselves—in our own eyes if nowhere else. We needed to pull off a coup.

The idea came from Steve. He marched into our room one night. Bob and I were sitting at our desks trying to work out some problem in physics. Actually, I was *trying* to work it out while Bob *was* working it out. Bob Porter was what was known as a whip. He, along with my best friend, Dick Kashnow, were head and shoulders above the rest of us when it came to physics. In our sophomore year, Bob transferred to MIT, an appropriate move for one of his caliber. I never heard from him again.

"I've got it," Steve announced.

"Well then don't come near me," Bob quickly retorted.

"No," Steve replied, "I've got a great idea!"

"An idea for what?" I asked.

"An idea for a sign snatch," said Steve impatiently.

"Well," said Bob, "let's have it."

"Here," said Steve, tossing a folded road map on Bob's desk.

Bob picked it up with me looking over his shoulder. "It's a map of Connecticut," he reported. "What's in Connecticut?"

"Open it up," said Steve.

Bob did so, laying the open map on his desk.

"So . . ." I chimed in.

"So look," said Steve.

Bob and I slid our eyes over the map. Bob saw it first. There, in upper central Connecticut was a town that had been circled by a red marking pen.

"Burlington," Bob read. "What's so special about Burlington?"

"Yeah," I echoed. "What's so special about Burlington?"

"Look harder," said Steve, a grin spreading over his face. We looked again. And again, Bob was the first to see it. Actually, I never did see it. I was totally in the dark. All I heard was "Wow!" When I looked down at Bob, he was staring intently at the map, a clone of Steve's grin spreading over his face.

"What?" I said, still lost.

"That's cool," said Bob as he started laughing.

"What?" I said.

"Isn't it?" said Steve.

"What?" I said.

"We've gotta get it," said Bob.

"What?" I said. At this moment, my two friends realized that I was somewhere out in the pasture behind left field.

"Look," said Bob, thrusting the map at me.

"Look at what?" I replied, starting to get a little annoyed. "All I see is Burlington circled in red. So what?"

"So look at the roads going into Burlington."

Again, I studied the map intently. "Well," I finally reported, "there's Route 4 going through Burlington east-west and Route 69 coming up from the south and ending in Burlington."

"YES!" screamed Steve, his eyes wide with excitement. "You've got it!"

"Got what?" I countered. "I have no idea what you're talking about."

"Sixty-nine!" shouted Bob and Steve in unison, both grinning, Cheshire-like.

"So it's Route 69," I replied. "So what?"

Bob and Steve turned toward one another, grins fading. "I don't think he knows what it means," says Steve.

"Of course he does," Bob defended. "Don't you?"

At this point, I was starting to feel a little ill at ease. I had absolutely no idea what was going on. Something that my two friends seemed to know so much about had completely gone over my head. But, of course, in those days, lots went over my head. The year was 1960, but I was still living in 1955. In fact, I was as far from the 60s as I was from the moon. If one received college credit for naiveté, I would have already earned my Ph.D. Hell, I was the East Coast distributor of naiveté. I had been going steady for a year and a half, and I had probably kissed her by then, but as far as anything else was concerned, well, let's just say that I spent a lot of time with my hands in my pockets. That's just the way it was at that time and place.

"No," I said softly, hoping that no one would hear me.

"Christ," said Steve. "You're a disgrace to New York. Where have you been all your life?"

"Lighten up," Bob interjected. "It's like this . . ." he continued in a fatherly fashion, turning his attention to me. Thirty seconds later he was finished. He stopped and looked at me, smiling. I wasn't smiling.

"You're kidding," I said.

"No," Bob replied, smile fading. "No, I'm not."

All at once, I was swimming in a sea of déjà vu so thick that it was threatening to suffocate me . . .

I was twelve years old, sitting in my bedroom, and my mother walked in with some books in her hand.

"Here," she said. "I want you to read these." And then she was gone.

I grabbed the top one eagerly. She was always bringing me great science fiction books from the library. But this wasn't science fiction. At first I thought it was, it was strange enough to be, but as I read, I realized, impossible as it seemed, that the author was serious. When, some unknown time later, I was finished reading, I took the books and put them outside my bedroom door. I wanted to get as far away from them as I could. I felt disgusted, even nauseated.

It was depressing to think that nature, an entity that I was at that time in my life learning to love and respect, had come up with such a foul plan.

"I'm never gonna do THAT!" I said to myself. Some time later, I changed my mind.

Now, six years later, I'm standing in my college dorm room looking into the eyes of my roommate Bob Porter who had just brought those books back into the room.

"Oh," I said, having no other sensible reply.

"Well, now you know. I think we should snatch one—it would be soooo cool. No one has anything like it."

"Yeah," Steve chimed in, "I'm ready right now."

At this point, I was only half present. Deep in thought, I was trying to appear *cool*, but I was unnerved. Do people really do things like that? Will I have to do that? Is it remotely possible that I would want to do that? What would Broni think about that? Is it possible that she is aware of that sort of thing?

"Well, are you coming?"

I had been so lost in my thoughts that I had lost track of the conversation. In those few moments, Steve and Bob had elected to drive to Connecticut to liberate one of the Route 69 signs. Steve was headed out the door to get Lee, and Bob was pulling on his pants (Bob always did his homework in his underwear; he claimed that he couldn't think when fully clothed).

"Well, are you coming?" asked Bob, as he pulled on the second leg.

"You're going to Connecticut . . . now?" This was the last thing that I wanted to do. I had homework, and it was already after 10 p.m. But, mostly, I didn't even want to think about the number 69.

"How far is it?" I asked.

"Not far—about eighty miles," Bob replied.

The truth is that it wasn't far. We were always jumping in the car and driving somewhere for no good reason at all. I remember one weekend in particular. My parents had been up to Worcester visiting me. They left about 4:00 p.m. to make the four-hour trip back to New York. A few of us were chatting in my dorm room after they left. Someone made the off-hand remark that it would be funny if my parents found us sitting in their living room when they got home. They had a thirty-minute head start, but they were going to stop for dinner. Well, we did it. It was a good joke, and it only cost us eight hours and $3.50 for gas. Another time we drove to NYC just to get some pizza at John's in the Village.

"Well, are ya comin'?" asked Bob, standing at the doorway searching his pockets for keys.

I was trapped between my gut feelings and my desire not to look foolish in front of my friends. Also weighing heavily was the admonition of our Pledgemaster, Mark Britnisky: "You guys are a team. You do things together! Never hang a brother out to dry." I was part of the team. In fact, I was one of the team leaders. In two months, I would be chosen Pledge of the Year, and in my senior year, I would be elected president of the fraternity. (In truth, the real leader of our class was my friend Dick. The only reason that I was elected president was because he did not want the office.) In those days, I believed that the way to best lead was to find out what the group wanted and take that as your task. I not only didn't follow my star, I had no idea what my star was. So I had to follow other people's stars.

"I'm coming," I said. "Let's go!" I grabbed my jacket and in five minutes the four of us were in the VW driving down the still sign-less Institute Road, heading for the Mass Pike.

The eighty-mile trip took us about two hours. We would have made it faster under ordinary conditions, but it was night and the last thirty miles or so were on narrow, unfamiliar roads.

We drove into Burlington at about 2:00 a.m. It was a smallish town, a main street with three traffic lights and several side streets intersecting the main street. The stores were closed, and the streets were empty. We glided past the city hall, the fire station and the police station. There was no sign of life. As we approached the second traffic light, we saw a sign: "Route 69—Turn Left." We had reached our goal. Victory was within sight.

We drove out of town, southbound on Route 69. It would not do to make the snatch in too populated an area. It was an act best carried out in rural darkness. As we drove we noted the route signs. They were spaced about a mile apart. At first, all that we passed were inappropriate. They were either too near a light or a residence. With so many signs, there was no need to take a risk. When we were about six miles out of town, there was an abrupt change. Gone were the houses and the lights. All our headlamps revealed was a tree-lined road stretching into the distance and disappearing into the darkness. This was exactly what we were looking for. The goal was at hand.

Within half a mile we found our sign. It stood in darkness. There were no houses or structures of any kind nearby. It had "Take Me" written all over it.

There was no need for conversation. There was no need to make a plan. We had done this many times before, and we each knew our role. We were professionals. Bob stopped the car in front of the sign, and the rest of us jumped out. I ran around to the front of the car and opened the trunk. I pulled out the box of tools, handed it to Lee, and slammed the lid. As the three of us walked towards the sign, Bob drove off.

We had decided long ago that a car parked by the roadside could attract attention. Also, while a person could duck down if a car passed, a vehicle was difficult to hide. So the plan was that Bob would drive up and down the road, passing us each time, and when we had "liberated" the sign we would signal him with a flashlight as he passed.

We walked to the sign, which was bolted about seven feet up on a metal post. Lee put the box of tools on the ground at the base of the post and pulled out the flashlight. It took only a moment to see that we had a problem.

There were four large bolts fastening the sign to the metal posts, and each bolt was covered by a thick layer of rust. From experience we knew that it would take less time to find another sign than to fight with these bolts. Bob was already about a quarter mile away from us, so there was nothing to do but wait for him to come back. Our agreement was always that he would drive out a mile, turn around, come back, pass us, head out a mile in the other direction, turn around again, and so on, until he saw our signal light. He would then stop and we would all pile in. This strategy had worked well for us.

So that we would not be seen by any passing vehicles, we stepped back farther from the roadside and over an embankment into a gully. Bob would be back in three or four minutes, so the discomfort of the hard, sloped ground was not an issue.

We chatted, making no effort to put a damper on our volume. Obviously there was no one nearby.

The minutes ticked by.

At about the five-minute mark, Lee commented, "He's late."

No one replied.

Another five minutes passed before we saw the headlamps in the distance.

"Here he is," I said, picking the flashlight off the ground. "I'll flag him down. Wait here."

I scrambled up the side of the gully and walked the ten yards or so to the roadside. Bob was within an eighth of a mile now, so I switched on the flashlight and waved it in his direction.

At first, there was no response, as if he didn't see the light. Then, the car slowed and angled over until it was pointing directly at me, placing me squarely in the headlamp beam. Immediately, a third, more powerful, light fell on me. It came from the driver's side of the car. I was now totally blinded by the lights.

My first thought was that Bob was fooling around.

My second thought was that I didn't remember that Bob had a searchlight bolted to the side of his car.

My third thought was the realization that this was not Bob. I was frozen, both from fear and blindness. I heard the door of the car open, and a command rang out.

"Stand where you are!"

Before I could even attempt to move, two figures descended upon me from out of the glare. One of them held a flashlight, which he pointed at me—a fourth beam to illuminate my terror.

"What are you doing here?"

"Uh, uh, just waiting for my friend to pick me up," I stammered.

"Is your friend the one in the VW bug just down the road?" demanded the voice.

"Y-Y-Yes," I managed.

"Well, you and your friend are both under arrest on suspicion of grand theft."

I felt my legs get weak, and I might have fallen had it not been for the two strong hands, one grabbing me from each side, which took my arms and led me to the car that had been illuminating me.

Now that I was out of the beam path, I could see that I had flagged down a Connecticut Highway Patrol car. I could also now see the faces of the two highway patrolmen who were guiding me forcefully toward the right rear door of the car. One of the officers opened the door while the other quickly ran his hands over my body, feeling for weapons. Once satisfied, he guided me into the back of the car. As I fell back into the seat, the dome light of the car illuminated the silver nameplate on the right pocket of the patrolman's uniform: Officer Frank Householder. Strange to say, with all that was going on, what went through my mind was, "Interesting name."

After they put me in the patrol car, the two officers got back into the front seat and the car started driving north, toward Burlington. The driver of the car, Householder, seemed to be in charge. He started asking me questions: my name, address, what we were doing in Burlington.

Through all the questioning, Householder was calm and soft-spoken. Calm, at least, until I started to answer the last question. When I said that the four of us had driven to Burlington from Worcester Tech to get a Route 69 road sign,

Householder brought the car to a rapid stop. He turned and looked at me.

"Do you mean that there are two more of you out there?"

"Yes," I said without hesitation. In the last few minutes, I had decided that in the current situation complete honesty was necessary. Maybe if we were cooperative, they would be lenient.

"Where are the other two?" Householder demanded.

"Back where you picked me up," I said softly. "They're hiding in the gully next to the sign."

Before I even finished the sentence, Householder had swung the car 180 degrees and headed back in the direction of the aborted crime scene. At the same time he picked up the car radio and requested a backup. As we drove back toward the sign, I sat in the back seat feeling a growing sense of doom.

As we approached the site, Householder slowed the car.

"Where are they?" he demanded.

"Up ahead . . . on the right . . . next to that route sign in that gully," I replied in a hoarse whisper.

"THIS IS THE POLICE. WE KNOW YOU'RE THERE. WE HAVE YOUR FRIENDS. COME ON OUT AND KEEP YOUR HANDS WHERE WE CAN SEE THEM."

After Steve and Lee were taken away in the second patrol car, Householder, who was still behind the wheel, turned to me.

"All right," he said, "Let's take care of you."

He pulled the car over to the right side of the road and turned off the engine. He turned in his seat until he was halfway facing me.

"Where did you stash the stuff?" he demanded.

"What?" I said, startled and confused.

"The parts that you and your friends got from the break-in—where did you stash them?"

Did I hear him correctly? Did he say break-in? I felt as though I were under water. The walls of the car seemed to close in on me.

"What?" I repeated stupidly.

"It will go easier on you if you tell us the truth now," Householder's partner interjected.

"I don't know anything about any parts or break-in. We just came down here to get a Route 69 sign. That's all."

Householder turned back to the wheel and started the car. "Well," he said as he resumed driving north, "we have four of you now. We'll get the truth from one of you."

Within ten minutes we arrived at the police station that we had passed earlier in the night, only now it was alive with activity. Three police cars were clustered around the entrance to the station, and most of the lights in the building were illuminated.

Householder pulled the car up beside the other three. I was taken from the car and led into the station to a room containing only two chairs and a lamp hanging from the ceiling. They sat me down in one of the chairs and left the room. They let me sit there stewing for about fifteen minutes. Finally, the door opened and Householder walked in accompanied by another man in plain clothes.

With Householder watching silently, the second man proceeded to question me all over again. He asked my name, place of residence, reason for being in Burlington on this night, and where we had hidden the parts. I answered all his questions in as honest and straightforward a manner as I could. As I was pleading ignorance as to the whereabouts of the missing parts, the door opened and another man walked in. He went over to the man in plain clothes and whispered into his ear. Then he left, followed by the interrogator and Householder. I was alone again.

Five minutes later, Householder came back. His demeanor had changed. He seemed more relaxed. A hint of a smile played around his lips as he said, "Come with me, Mr. Waxman." He led me to an adjacent room. In it was a large table surrounded by about a dozen chairs. Sitting at the table were Bob, Steve, and Lee.

"Take a seat," Householder said easily.

"I suppose you boys would like to know what went down here tonight?"

The four of us nodded in unison.

"Well, it seems that about the time you boys drove through Burlington, two men broke into Blake's Auto Parts shop and stole several thousand dollars worth of VW parts. A witness saw them leaving in a late-model, light-colored VW Beetle. Naturally, when we saw you and your VW cruising up and down 69, we were suspicious. But when we separated you, and you all told us the same screwy story about driving almost 200 miles to steal a Route 69 sign, we started having our doubts. Your story was too ridiculous to be made up.

"And then, about half an hour ago, two men in a VW were arrested in Hartford. Their car was filled with auto parts with the Blake's label on them. One of our men is now on his way to Hartford to bring them back. I think we can safely say that we have our perpetrators.

"But now about you boys," he said, becoming sterner. "You're lucky that we took you in before you stole the sign. If you had a stolen sign in your possession when we picked you up, well . . . well, you don't want to go there. You boys were lucky this time, but you may not be the next. I suggest that you go back to Worcester, put your energy into your studies, and leave signs where they belong. Now get out of here!"

"Yes sir," we said, almost in unison, as we scrambled to our feet and walked rapidly toward the exit door.

In two minutes we were driving east on Route 4 out of Burlington and into the countryside. It was just getting light when we drove onto the WPI campus. We would just have time to shower before breakfast. We were exhausted but we had our 8:00 a.m. calculus class to attend, followed by five other classes. It would be a long day.

Bob pulled into the same spot he had vacated seven hours before. He got out of the car, walked around to the front and opened the trunk lid so that we might claim our jackets. He stood there, looking into the trunk with a puzzled expression on his face.

"What's wrong?" asked Lee.

"There's a road sign in here. Was it here when we started?"

"No," I said, "the trunk was empty."

"Well, it's not empty now," said Bob as he pulled out the sign.

We put the sign, an obvious gift from Officer Frank Householder, on my bureau where the Institute Rd sign that started the whole affair had once resided. We had headed out in search of a sign that said "69." What we got instead was a sign we could leave up when our parents came to visit. We also got a dose of old fashioned morality courtesy of the Connecticut Highway Patrol.

The sign said:

CHURCH AHEAD

Strangers in a Strange Land

*I*n the summer of 1954, I almost died by falling down a six-story incinerator shaft. That event, however, was a distant second to the real near-death experience of that summer, an experience that was, surprisingly, perpetrated by my parents.

Since I was thirteen that year, I was to have my Bar Mitzvah, the ancient Jewish, male rite-of-passage. Because hunting wild boar is forbidden within the city limits of Brooklyn, I had to demonstrate my manhood by performing some equally excruciating, dangerous and terrifying act of bravado. I was told at age nine that I was to spend the next four years—two hours a day, five days a week—in training so that at the end of that apprenticeship, on a Saturday near my birthday in July of 1954, I would be able to stand on the altar of the temple of the Flatbush Jewish Center and there, in front of all my friends and relatives, read a segment of the Torah in Hebrew. When I was taken to Hebrew School for the first-day registration, I told my parents, "Thank you very much, but I think I'll pass on this one." But they said, "You're going!" I begged and pleaded, but they said, "You're going!" I screamed and cried, but they said, "You're going!" In the end, I went.

I believe that I was, possibly, the worst Hebrew student in the history of the Flatbush Jewish Center. I couldn't memorize the alphabet; I couldn't pronounce the words; I couldn't sing the songs. The only thing that I remember from my four-year tour of duty at FJC was that one day my teacher bent a six-inch nail with his bare hands. He had boasted of his strength and challenged us to bring him a spike for the demonstration. As my father had a well-equipped workshop, I had no difficulty in locating the item and brought it to school the next day. (These days, such an act would get me expelled. If I had realized the potential, I would have carried it around my neck on a chain instead of in a paper sack.) Sure enough, there in front of the class, he bent the nail in half. In that moment, I learned the only piece of information that I retained from three years of study: Don't screw around with Mr. Teitlebaum.

At the end of my third year of Hebrew school, even my parents had to admit that I was getting nowhere. My Bar Mitzvah was less than a year away, and I was no closer to being able to read the Torah than I was on the day that I was born. At this rate, when it came time for me to stand on the altar and say something, someone was going to be very embarrassed, and that someone was going to be everybody.

In an act of desperation, my parents hired a private Hebrew tutor to come to the house each week to help me with my lessons. He, astute fellow that he was, quickly realized that I knew no Hebrew at all and that I had no chance of learning any for the rest of my life, let alone in the few months remaining before my show hit the road. He, therefore, did the only sensible thing; he wrote out my required section of the Torah phonetically in English so that I might spend the next ten months memorizing the sounds. I would sit and look at page after page of meaningless sounds and combinations of sounds: "BO-RUCH A-TOH A-DO-NOY, E-LO-HAY-NOO ME-LECH HO-O-LOM . . . ." I spent month after month memorizing useless belches and guttural utterances, having not the slightest clue as to what I was saying. Camus and Sartre would have appreciated my situation.

As my Saturday in July approached, the panic within me grew. There was no doubt in my mind that I was going to make a complete fool of myself and that my parents would hate me forever. I begged and pleaded for a reprieve—promised to do anything necessary to pay off my debt to God in some other manner. I would continue to go to temple for 100 years if they would just allow me to be in some other country on July 17th. It was all to no avail. The caterer had already been hired. My fate was sealed.

I do not remember anything that occurred on that day until I walked down off the altar. My only explanation is that I was so frozen with fear that my neurons could not effect an electrical memory pattern in my brain cells; I was experiencing organic superconductivity. But when I left the altar—that was a different story! My life had started again! I was going to live! The world was a joyous place! The first person to greet me at the end of the service was my friend Myles. We embraced and jumped up and down a little. He told me that I did a great job, and though I knew that he was lying (he was a good friend; one of only two I had who never tried to hurt me in any way), I didn't care. It was over!

I spent the rest of the day celebrating as an adult male. I ate six pieces of pickled herring (in sour cream, of course), two corned beef sandwiches, one tongue sandwich, ten slices of stuffed derma, and an unknown number of Ebinger's petite fours. I also smoked two white Owl cigars and drank three rye & ginger ales. Finally, I capped it off by throwing up four times.

As for the temple, I never went back—that is, not for 46 years. In the summer of 2000, Albey and I decided to revisit the old neighborhood. We met our old elementary school chum, Alan Greenburg, in front of P.S. 130 and together we did the neighborhood. We entered the school and were shown around by the principal. We went to the Parade Grounds where we used to play ball. We went to the soda shop and had an egg cream (maybe two egg creams). And we went to Church Avenue, the location of two of the most defining places of my youth: the Beverly Movie Theater and the Flatbush Jewish Center. The day so far had been a joy. I loved visiting all of the old places. Everyone we had met had been so friendly, especially when we explained that we had lived in the neighborhood in the 50s. And the whole place looked good, well taken care of. The anticipation of what was to come next buoyed me. As we approached the FJC, I felt my excitement grow. At long last I was going to exorcise the demon that had been plaguing me for almost fifty years. I was going to wash away all of those negative thoughts and nightmarish memories. I was going to make peace with the FJC. As we walked up Church Avenue toward Ocean Parkway, I turned and said to Albey, "Ya know, this is the first time in my life that I am looking forward to going into this place. I'm really excited!"

But as the Center came into sight, we noticed that the tenor of the neighborhood had changed. It had been completely taken over by Orthodox Jews. Men in long black coats and young males sporting "pais" abounded. We climbed the steps to the temple but found the door locked. We knocked, heard footsteps approaching, and a man in a black suit appeared in the doorway. We explained to him that we had both been Bar Mitzvahed at this place forty-six years ago, that we were revisiting the old neighborhood, and that we wanted to revisit the temple. He looked us up and down suspiciously, almost certainly taking exception to our attire, which consisted of sneakers, jeans and T-shirts, the same clothes we wore all those years ago to go to Hebrew school.

"Go away!" he said curtly and slammed the door in our faces.

Solar Eclipse

$\mathcal{W}$hen I was a young boy in Brooklyn, I knew of the occurrence of solar eclipses but had no chance to observe one. In fact, my first opportunity to view a total solar eclipse came in 1970, when I was twenty-eight years old. In January of that year, I was still a graduate student in astronomy at UCLA. One day, one of my friends, John Mottman, came to me and asked if I would like to drive with him and Bruce Bohannon, a fellow graduate student, to see the total solar eclipse that would occur on March 7. The rub was that the path of totality would sweep across Mexico south of the city of Oaxaca, a drive of almost 2,000 miles from Los Angeles (each way!). When I went home and told my wife Broni of the invitation, I was surprised to discover that she was in favor of it and, moreover, wanted to come along. In the end, we decided that John and Bruce would drive in one car and Broni, our son Keith, our dog Charley, and I would drive in another. We planned to drive in tandem, so that if one of the cars had difficulty, help would be nearby.

On February 25, about ten days before the eclipse, our small caravan left Los Angeles and headed southward to the Imperial Valley and across the border into Mexico. It was the first time I had been in a foreign country (Canada, as everyone knows, is not a foreign country) and every moment was an adventure. I was entranced by the desert scenery, the quaint villages, the strange language, the currency, and the simple poverty. The people were friendly, curious and helpful. Because Broni knew Spanish, she took the lead in helping us get around. It was a new set of roles for us—she the leader, I the follower.

Over the next ten days, we wended our way down the Mexican coastal highway, through places with such, for me, strange names as Hermosillo, Guaymas, Mazatlan and Guadalajara. It was off-season, so the roads and cities were virtually empty. The Saguaro deserts were limitless, foreboding and, at the same time, inviting. We would park our van and go running off among the cacti, throwing sticks for Charley and balls for Keith. The sensation that most gripped me was one of alien loneliness combined with expectations of impending adventure. I felt as though I were in a fantasy, exploring with John Carter the sands of Mars or perhaps traveling alongside Fred C. Dobbs on a quest for gold.

On the fifth of March we arrived in Oaxaca. In spacetime, we were about thirty miles and two days from our appointment with the moon's shadow. Over the previous eight days, we had watched as the waning orb slid from near-full through quarter and had reached, finally, a thin crescent phase. We could see before our eyes the unfolding of the event that was to come, and, although none of us had witnessed a total solar eclipse before and had only reports to guide us as to what to expect, we could feel great expectation and excitement welling within.

We spent the day in Oaxaca, sitting in the plaza drinking Cokes (we heard that they were safe), visiting the street markets (too cautious to eat anything) and tramping the ruins at Montealban. As we were now near the centerline, humanity was more in abundance and a party atmosphere prevailed.

Tour busses (generally from the States) could be seen cruising the town and parked in the lots adjacent to the ancient ruins. New cars with U.S. license plates now seemed as common as the old, smoking, sidewinding vehicles that characterized the traffic since we had crossed the border at Mexicali. This activity was a harsh interruption of the tranquility and isolation that we had so enjoyed in the desert. That experience had been so soul-satisfying that the contrast of Oaxaca was jarring. It was absolutely unthinkable to view the eclipse in the company of hordes of people and the concomitant din. We resolved to leave the main road, abandon our original site plan, and head off into the mountains.

In the early morning of the seventh of March, we drove to the town of Miahuatlan, found a narrow road that headed into the hills and started driving up. At about 8:00 a.m., we arrived at the top of a peak, probably about 8,000 feet in elevation, from which one could see for miles.

An unobstructed view, particularly towards the west, is essential for eclipse viewing. Since the moon orbits the earth from west to east, the shadow of the moon will approach an eclipse watcher from the west. If one is on high ground (and we were), it is possible, in the moments before totality, to see the shadow moving toward your position.

This shadow possesses two special characteristics. First, it is wide—generally between 100 and 150 miles in diameter. This makes it appear more like a wall of darkness than a circular spot. Second, it is moving very fast. The exact speed depends on the latitude of the eclipse path; in our case, the shadow speed was about 1,000 miles per hour. These two characteristics, from what we had heard, make the oncoming shadow well worth observing, and this was why we sought high ground with a western exposure.

By 9:00 a.m. we had our equipment set up. We had each come with various forms of devices, both audio and video, to record the spectacle. My task was to shoot both 8mm and 16mm movies of the eclipse. These films, as well as telescopic photos taken by John and Bruce, were to serve as the core for a documentary film of the trip that we planned to create. (Ultimately, we did make the film and, crude though it is, I view it from time to time just to remember).

As I recall it now, the partial phases of the eclipse were to start at about 10:00 a.m. At the time I knew the moment of first contact, as it is called by astronomers, to less than one second. I can remember sitting on the ground with maps and charts, making hand calculations (no calculators in those days) based on our best guess latitude and longitude. There was really no good reason for us to know first contact to within a second, but we were astronomers and that's what astronomers do. I guess it gives us the illusion of understanding—perhaps even controlling—nature.

At the appointed moment, the disk of the moon made contact with the sun. The event itself is not particularly spectacular; in fact, it's hard to really tell that anything has happened. If you're looking at the sun through a telescope (using a solar filter, of course), you see a slight dimple in the smooth curve of the solar limb or edge. As you watch, the dimple gets wider and deeper as the moon intrudes further into the Earth-sun line of sight. Viewed with the naked eye (also though a filter) the event is so gentle that it takes a few minutes of lunar intrusion to be certain that anything has happened at all.

First contact generally elicits cries of delight and excitement, not because it looks like anything, but rather, because it means something. It is like a trumpeter signaling the approach of a royal procession, only in this case, the procession is a

100-mile wide shadow, now about 1,000 miles distant to the west, bearing down on us at 1,000 miles per hour.

As the next hour passed, the moon slid ever more deeply over the face of the sun. This progress, now easily followed with our hand-held filters, seemed, at first, to have little effect on the surrounding terrestrial environment. A little bit of sun goes a long way. By thirty minutes after first contact, however, we could sense subtle changes. First, it became cooler. Before first contact, the air temperature on this high, exposed peak had climbed to above 80 degrees. Now it had fallen back into the 70s. We could detect a visual change, too. The sky and landscape now seemed slightly hazy, as though a layer of thin cirrus clouds had intruded into this otherwise perfect day. Yet, a glance at the sky reassured that no clouds were on hand.

Over the next thirty minutes these two effects deepened and were joined by a third—wind. Veteran eclipse watchers expect eclipse winds. We, of course, knew nothing about them. Since the temperature in the umbral spot (which is what astronomers call the moon's shadow) is considerably lower than the temperature outside of the spot, there is a significant pressure difference between inside and outside. This pressure difference results in wind.

As the moment of totality approached, the natural visage resembled nothing so much as an impending storm; the air temperature had become noticeably chilly; the winds were picking up; and daylight was failing—rapidly. In the distance, a rooster was crowing, and one of us remarked that animals, too, might have lore pertaining to eclipses.

At this point, two or three minutes before totality, I remember feeling a fleeting panic. I realized that I had made a mistake. I had come to this eclipse as a scientist, armed with cameras, films, tripods, drive motors and the like. I was above nature, outside the event, gazing down with fatherly interest and curiosity. I had come to capture the eclipse, to master it, tame it and bring it back to civilization for display. But now, in those ephemeral moments before we were engulfed, I realized the truth. Everything was out of control. Nature, in a display of her great power and intent, was silently thundering across the earth, and I was standing in the way. Rather than being the observer, I was the subject, and all of my plans, desires, wishes, hopes and wants made no damn bit of difference. I saw this small, stupid, puny animal standing on a mountain peak, fiddling with some metal boxes, thinking that it knew something about something while all the while this incredible wave of darkness was bearing down, engulfing all in its path, at 1,000 miles an hour. It was all insane.

"There it is!" screamed Bruce, a touch of panic in his voice. I jerked my head upward from my camera and looked toward the west. There it was indeed. A full minute before totality, fifteen miles away, the wall of darkness appeared. It stretched from north to south. There was absolutely no sense of it being a finite spot a mere one hundred miles across. As far as I could tell, it could have been infinite in length. I could see it approaching, rolling over the hills and valleys, eating forests and fields as it came. Even today, I can still feel the terror of that sight. I was educated. I was a scientist. I had purposely traveled 2,000 miles for this moment and, yet, an older, species-wise part of me wanted to turn and run toward the east, to escape the doom that this wall of darkness must surely bring. In an instant, I understood the reason for the eclipse stories that have been passed to us—why ancient or primitive peoples would take this sight as a prelude to the end of the world. I would never again be amused by these stories.

As the shadow silently roared across the last large valley before reaching our exposed, and thus precarious, perch, I felt suddenly dizzy and disoriented. Before I had a chance to even wonder why, the answer became clear. Rolling across the ground (and up our bodies and across the cars and up the trees) were eastward moving, alternating bands of light and dark. Later, upon sober reflection, it seemed to me that they were generally linear, about two feet wide and moving at about twenty miles per hour. At the time, however, I felt as though I were at the bottom of a swimming pool with the ripples on the surface above me casting strange shadows on the pool bottom. The vertigo produced by these waves (astronomers call them shadow bands and no complete explanation for them is at hand) was so strong that I immediately dropped down to the ground and sat there, watching, for what seemed like minutes, the waves of light and dark wash over my arms and legs. (The tape of our conversation later demonstrated that the duration was only about five to ten seconds).

I had been thrust into an alien, ineffable universe. It was day, but it wasn't. It was clear, but it wasn't. I was outside, but I wasn't. I was all alone, sitting on a hilltop in some parallel universe, wondering how I had gotten there and what to do next.

My stupor was interrupted by John's voice. "Diamond ring! Filters off!" I had been so awestruck by the approaching shadow and its accompanying bands that I had totally forgotten about the sun. Without caution (I was beyond caring at that point) I turned my head upward to where the sun had been a minute before, but it was gone. It wasn't that that part of the sky was empty. It was just that the thing I saw there wasn't the sun. In its place was a hole in the sky circled by blue-white rays of luminous intensity. The rays seemed to radiate from the edge of the hole and were alive with motion; they shimmered and danced as though engaged in a tribal rite. At one point on the rim, the circle was interrupted by an intense splash of light, too bright to stare into directly. Whatever this thing was, it wasn't the sun! Whatever it was, it was awesome! Again, as had happened not thirty seconds before, I was frozen. The oncoming shadow had been terrifying. The shadow bands had been disorienting. The diamond ring was magnificent. I remember saying nothing but our tape-recorded, "Oh God, look at that!"

Of course we knew about the diamond ring effect, the last splash of sun to be seen as the moon, perfectly matched in angular size, inserts itself directly in the observer's line of sight. And, certainly, we knew that the ring creating the illusion of a hole was the first appearance of the magical corona, the two-million-degree hot outer atmosphere of the sun and the quest of our two-thousand-mile journey. Yes, we knew all these things, but it didn't matter. This had nothing to do with knowledge or science or even thinking. This was pure, raw, primal feeling. I was an animal without a brain, and this incredible natural event was being infused directly into the core of my being without cerebral filtration or interpretation.

As we watched over a period of seconds, the diamond shrunk, and as the last vestiges of solar limb disappeared behind the moon, the entire ring erupted into a string of explosions of light. The explosions, each lasting about a second before fading, looked as though a Fourth of July celebration had been staged to herald the onset of totality. The only thing missing was the audible pop.

Baily's beads, as these flashes are called, are often seen at the start and end of totality, as light from the solar limb passes through mountain valleys on the moon's edge. The quality of the apparition depends on the geometry of the particular eclipse and, from my experience with later eclipses, the beads we saw were exceptional.

"Jerry, are we running?" Bruce's voice brought me back. I had totally forgotten about my cameras and mission. If it hadn't been for the motor drives, I would have blown the whole thing. I checked through the viewfinders and saw that the sun was centered in the fields of both cameras. I also noticed that, through the camera, the sun looked just as it did in any photo or film; it looked like a total solar eclipse. Satisfied that I was being a good scientist, I turned my head once more upward toward the spectacle. What I saw was not what I had seen through the viewfinder. It was a totally different event, a universe apart.

When I was a little boy, my parents took me to visit the airships that were housed at Lakehurst, New Jersey. I had seen these giant, cigar-shaped balloons slowly crossing the space over my house in Brooklyn, and I had seen a film of what had happened to the Hindenburg, so I was excited at the prospect of seeing one of these great ships in person. Actually, after seeing the Hindenburg footage, I wasn't certain that I wanted to get too near a potential inferno, but my parents explained to me the difference between hydrogen and helium, so my concerns were allayed.

The trip to Lakehurst was memorable. The airships were larger than I had ever imagined and we saw many, but the most impressive sight for me was when we entered a hangar that was housing no airship. The hangars we had previously visited were occupied by ships and so were relegated to gray, unimportant background. Here, there was nothing but the hangar, and for the first time I got a sense of their size. I thought that I knew how big a building could be, but I had been wrong. This place was immense. In the light from the open door, the walls seemed to fade upward toward a ceiling that, because of its distance from the ground, could not be seen in detail. The far wall of the structure was, it seemed, several football fields away and, therefore, indistinct. Then someone closed the door.

At first, it seemed totally dark but after a moment, as my eyes adjusted, I realized that there was light coming from above. On the ceiling there was a small, blue-white light. It was the sole light in the hanger, and its cold glow struggled to fill the cavernous space. Now, the ceiling, save for the bulb, could not be seen and neither could the distant walls. I knew that I was inside a structure, but I couldn't see the structure. It felt as though I were outside while being inside, and the outside was presided over by a sun gone wrong—a dim, blue parody of the sun we know. I have been carrying this image since childhood.

My first glimpse of totality flashed me back to that hangar in Lakehurst. There, hanging in the sky of this alien planet, was the blue-white bulb, its dim light weakly illuminating the hangar that was, I hoped, a hilltop in Mexico. I knew that I was outside, but all my senses told me that I was inside; the universe had become a giant enclosure.

But this bulb was not like the bulb in Lakehurst. The color was the same. The size was the same. The brightness was the same. This bulb, however, had depth and dynamism. It was more than four-dimensional in space and life; it had directions and freedoms that allowed it to exist, simultaneously, not only in Euclidean volume but in psychic volume as well. Its intrusion into my being was as real as a cinder in the eye with, however, the pain replaced by rapture. Moreover, it moved and changed form as I watched, first a hole in the sky with shimmering edges (is this how one travels out of the universe?), then a black diamond generating radiant energy from its periphery. It was never just the moon covering the sun; it was alien; it was magic; it was unknown and unknowable; it was infinite. It was over.

We had calculated the duration of totality to be three minutes and twenty-seven seconds—207 seconds during which time the moon's umbral shadow would pass over our location. These few seconds lasted an eternity and were over in an instant. As rapidly as it had approached, the shadow receded, an instant replay projected in negative time. Baily's beads, the diamond ring, shadow bands and the shadow retreated toward the eastern horizon, rushing toward an appointment with thousands of eclipse-watchers sitting on hilltops as were we, waiting for their moment out of the sun, then out to sea where hundreds of small craft were stationed to catch their piece of nature.

It was as a dream, real yet illusory, firm yet fleeting. What was that feeling? What was that thought? Did this really happen? As we gathered our equipment we jabbered excitedly, reporting what we had seen to our comrades as though they had not been there to see it for themselves and as though it were possible to tell what we had seen anyway. Within an hour, we had eaten lunch, packed up and were on our way northward. We had left the hilltop physically, but a part of my psyche was left behind. It is still there and will never leave.

For weeks afterward, as I lay in bed awaiting the arrival of sleep, the vision of the eclipsed sun would fill my waning consciousness and move in and out of my dreams. While I had been careful to use filters to protect my eyes from the photospheric rays, I had taken no such precaution with my soul. I was permanently inscribed.

When we returned to L.A., charged with excitement, we descended upon the eclipse catalog to plan our future adventures, and in the following years we went: July 10, 1972 on the Gaspé Peninsula; February 8, 1979 in Winnipeg; and "The Big One"—July 11, 1991, the day of my 50th birthday, at sea in the Gulf of California. One was weathered out, one was OK, and one was good, but none was remotely like that experience on the Mexican hilltop, and no eclipse I see in the future will be. First eclipses, like first loves, cannot be duplicated.

Eclipse Day—2006

 $\mathcal{T}$ he sky at the horizon took on that familiar shade of
crimson shading to vermilion that foretold of danger. The winds
whistled in agreement as they started whipping up the sand,
and the temperature dropped in concert with the lighting. As
the sky continued to darken, one could imagine hearing the
sound of the shadow as it swept toward us at some 1,500
miles per hour—a sort of shadowy, foreboding sound. I was
feeling a vague disquiet as Zero Hour approached.

Here we go again, I thought. Was I going to lose it as I
had the past two times? We would soon see. It was really
getting dark now—and quickly. I could see Venus and Mercury
alongside the sun. Just another few seconds . . . almost there . . .
aaannndd there's the diamond ring—the last vestige of the
sun sticking out from behind the moon.

"OOOOooooohhhhhh God! Oh My God! Jer, it's beautiful!"
squealed Kathleen, who was sitting on the asphalt next to me
on my right side. She had my arm in a death grip, digging in
her nails. I was immediately brought back to my first time on a
mountaintop in southern Mexico. It had struck me as strongly
as it was striking Kathleen now. I had felt that welling in my
chest as though it were going to burst. I had to take my mind
off of Kathleen's reaction before it was too late.

I looked over at Alisa and was about to ask a rather pedestrian question, but then I saw that look of rapture on her face, and I knew that I had better not disturb her. So I turned my attention back to Kathleen.

"See," I said, nodding knowingly. "I told you that this was great. But you have to see it to believe it. It can't be described."

"Woooww, you're right," said Kathleen, a bit dreamily. "Now I understand why people chase these things around the world. Damn, that's eerie." All the while, she was riveted on the sky.

"Did you see any shadow bands at second contact . . . or Bailey's Beads?"

"No," she said shaking her blond mop of hair, "I missed them."

"I don't think there were any to miss, at least I didn't see any," I volunteered. I had gotten a grip back on myself.

"Look at the red light all around the horizon," she said.

"That's the 360-degree sunrise that I was telling you about. It happens because the sun is shining about seventy-five miles away from here in all directions. Beautiful, isn't it?"

"It's fantastic!" she fairly shrieked.

We fell into silence—into our own thoughts. As the eclipse started coming to an end, playing the opening stages in reverse order, I started to feel my emotion welling up. I'm sure that it was Kathleen's reaction to the eclipse that did it. She was mirroring for me my own reaction to my first eclipse—a feeling that was so strong that I had traveled around the world four more times to try to recapture or at least understand it. I had been, to this point, unsuccessful.

Oh, damn it, I thought. You're not going to cry, are you? You're not going to make a fool of yourself in front of Kathleen and Alisa, not to mention the thousands of other people who are gathered here? But the harder I tried to choke back the sensation, the harder it hit me. Finally, as our almost four minutes out of the sun ended and third contact, signaling another diamond ring, was upon us, I could no longer hold back the tears—and they flowed. Kathleen just sat there, smiling at me, but giving me space to have my reaction. I think she understood what had just transpired even if she didn't understand her part in it.

And then I noticed that the guy with the TV camera about fifty feet away was pointing his camera at me. I could see that he was filming through his telephoto lens, so he must have been right in on my face—my, at that moment, crying face. I felt myself stiffen at the invasion of privacy this camera represented, but I realized I was a guest in their country. And, really, he was just doing his job. So I just let it be.

But then he walked over to his interviewer and whispered something to her. Now I had spoken to this woman before the eclipse. She was walking around the site, cameraman trailing, just talking to different people. She had first interviewed Alisa and then she had walked over to me. She asked if she could ask me a few questions for Egyptian TV, and I'd said "Yes." The interview had gone sort of like this:

Interviewer: Hi! What's your name?
JW: Jerry Waxman.
Int: Where are you from?
JW: California.
Int: That's a long way to come for four minutes.
JW: You obviously have not seen an eclipse before.
Int: No. I have not. Have you?
JW: Four or five.

Int: You have been to five eclipses. May I ask why?

JW: There are two parts to that answer.

Int: What are they?

JW: Well, the first part is that eclipses are the most beautiful natural phenomenon I have ever seen.

Int: And the second part?

JW: Well, the second part is totally ineffable. You'll have to see one to find out.

Int: Fair enough. Thank you.

And she had stood up and walked away, looking for another likely candidate and probably thinking that I was daft. Now, her attention was once again called to me—this time by her cameraman. She walked over to me, microphone leading.

Int: What are you feeling right now?

Kathleen (obviously sensing an invasion of privacy and trying to run interference for me):   Because he's an astronomer, he really likes these eclipses.

Int: You didn't tell me that you were an astronomer before.

JW: You didn't ask me before.

Int: You're right. You're obviously affected very much by this event. Why?

I was stuck. Try as I might, I could not think of a good answer to her question. I just sat there, looking at her. Finally, out of some desperation, I made something up about the way people were fouling this beautiful planet. It was quite lame.

When I finished, she thanked me and walked away. I was left alone with my thoughts. What had happened out there?

I had to figure it out. For my own well-being, I had to figure it out.

My task was simple. I merely had to figure out why eclipses were such an emotional thing for me—that is, why they were so important.

Well, why were they? Let's face it. They're beautiful, but not that beautiful. The Grand Canyon, Delicate Arch, and Niagara Falls I think are more beautiful than a total solar eclipse. Maybe it's the fact that they're rare. But are they rare? There certainly is a popular notion that they're rare.

Unfortunately (or fortunately), the truth is that they're not rare. In fact, there are two to five solar eclipses per year on Earth, half of which are total. The average width of the path of totality is 100 miles and its length is 5,000 miles. This means an area on the Earth of 500,000 square miles will see the eclipse. Since the entire surface area of the Earth is $(4)(3.14)(4000 \text{ mi.})^2 = 200$ million square miles (the surface area of a sphere is $4\pi r^2$, where r is the radius of the sphere), that's roughly 500,000/200,000,000, or 1/4 % of the entire surface (let's call it 1/8 % of the surface, adjusting for the fact that about half the surface is water). Assuming that the population is distributed uniformly, 1/8 % x 6 billion = 7 million people see, or are in a position to see, the eclipse. We should reduce this amount to five million to account for those people who find themselves along the eclipse path through no fault of their own, but because of ignorance, fear, or preoccupation, do not see it. We would be justified in adding to this number a factor to take into account all of the people who come into the path just for the purpose of seeing the eclipse. However, for the sake of conservatism, I will not do that.

At seven million people per eclipse, we have in ten years about seventy million people who have seen a total solar eclipse. How rare is that?

So, again I drew a blank. It wasn't aesthetics, and it wasn't rarity. I was beginning to worry that there was no rational explanation for it, or that I was just crazy about eclipses. But then it hit me . . . and it all made such exquisite sense. It was God!

I'll say it again to prove that it wasn't a typo. It was God!

Now, I know what you're thinking. You're thinking that scientists are not supposed to believe in God. Well, you're right—most don't. But they pay a heavy price for their disbelief. You see, human beings are the only animals (we know of) who know there are such things as a past and a future, and as such, they are the only ones who know they are going to die. This terrifies them so much that they are forced to make up a fairy tale in which they don't really die after all. That fairy tale is called God, or religion. Now, I know that what I'm saying is heresy, but just stop reacting a moment (if you are reacting) and use some critical thinking. Of all of the questions facing humans today, the one that is the least supported by factual evidence is the question of the existence of God. To my knowledge, not one shred of evidence exists that supports His existence. In fact, the definition of the word "faith" is belief in something in the absence of factual evidence. You can see why scientists, in the progress of their work, are forced to eschew faith and look for objective evidence. So, what does this all have to do with the connection between God and eclipses? Patience.

All of the foregoing puts scientists between a rock and a hard place because they're human too, and they also, secretly, wish to be lulled into the false sense of security provided by religion. So what do they do? Well, many scientists I know deify nature, something that is OK where they come from, and worship that. One could say that they become pagans of a sort—but there is a difference.

While a pagan might worship the sun or the moon, scientists do not do that. They are far too familiar with these objects, and you know what familiarity breeds. So, if not the sun and moon, what do scientists worship? The answer is that they worship ideas, such as that of an eclipse—what makes it happen, what makes it go. I believe that in the machinations that give rise to eclipses, astronomers have glimpsed the face of God.

Let's face it. On the surface of things, total solar eclipses are a pretty unlikely phenomenon. Let's look at what you have here. First, you need a satellite to pass in front of the sun. But just any size satellite will not do. It has to appear from the Earth slightly larger than the sun, so it blocks the photosphere, but not so large as to cut off the corona. Well, the moon fills the bill. It is precisely 400 times smaller than the sun and 400 times closer than the sun, so that they both appear as the same size, $1/2°$. What are the chances of a coincidence like that?

Being 1/400 the size of the sun makes the moon a very large satellite indeed. In fact, if you strip Pluto of its planet status, as the Hayden Planetarium of the American Museum of Natural History in New York has recently done, the moon takes the place of the largest satellite in the solar system, in relation to the size of the planet it is orbiting. And there are more than 100 satellites out there. Curious.

Even more curious is this: almost all of the satellites orbit their planet around its equator, a likely happenstance if the satellite is formed by accretion (condensing from gravity out of material left over after the formation of the planet). But as it is, the moon does not orbit the equator. It is tilted by between eighteen to twenty-eight degrees off the equator, and it is much more closely aligned with the ecliptic, or plane of the solar system (the moon orbits the Earth within five degrees of the plane of the ecliptic). The important point here is that this orbit plane for the moon pretty much negates accretion for the origin of the moon. It argues instead for some sort of capture from the plane of the solar system (because it is lying in the plane of the solar system). The problem with a capture hypothesis is that because of energy considerations, captures are difficult, indeed nearly impossible, to pull off.

This has led to a mini-crisis in astronomy, which has led to this highly problematic hypothesis: the "large impact hypothesis" in which the Earth is hit in the mantle by a Mars-sized body that combines with and blasts out a hunk of the Earth-projectile mixture. Part of the mixture is lost to space; part of the mixture falls to Earth. What did neither, falls into orbit around the Earth as the moon and continues to orbit until this day. This theory is sort of a combination of the capture hypothesis and the impact hypothesis, and it is necessary to fulfill all of the restrictions brought about by observations of the moon[11].

---

[11]   Two observations restrict the hypothesis: 1. The orbit of the moon lies closer to the plane of the ecliptic (5 degrees) than it does to the plane of the equator (18-28 degrees). This means that it is more likely that the moon came from the solar system—hence, a capture. 2. Moon rocks show that the composition of the moon is similar to the Earth except that it is depleted in iron. That is why we hypothesize a glancing impact off the mantle. The mantle, which mixes with the matter of the projectile, is deficient in iron.

Now, any astronomer will tell you that the above scenario for lunar formation is an exceedingly tricky business with no room for error. In other words, it would be a real golf shot. Who could make a shot like that?

Here's one more fact that I think is important: eclipses, as we see them, are for this time only. That's right. In the future there will be no more total solar eclipses. This is because of "tidal evolution." You see, the Earth and the moon are locked in a gravitational battle, fighting for control over the Earth's water. The moon pulling on the tidal bulge, in an attempt to capture the water, forces the water to roll backward over the speedily rotating Earth. The effect is to slow the rotation of the Earth by 0.002 seconds per century. In the language of Newtonian mechanics, the moon is causing an action to occur on Earth. The result is that, by the third law (action/reaction), the Earth has to put a reaction back on the moon. It does this by accelerating the moon in its orbit so that it slowly spirals away from the earth (at about one inch/year). In less than a billion years (your basic astronomical snap of the fingers), the moon will be too far away to cover the photosphere, and total solar eclipses will cease to occur.

So, coincidentally, we happen to live at a time on Earth when these magnificent eclipses occur. Or is it a coincidence? By the principle attributed to the Fourteenth Century English philosopher William of Occam, "Plurality should not be posited without necessity,"[12] I submit to you two theories of the origin of eclipses: one, that a fantastic series of coincidences and

---

[12]   This principle is sometimes referred to as the principle of "Occam's Razor," and it means that when you have competing theories, the one calling for the fewest assumptions is most likely to be true.

unlikely events led to their occurrence (the unlikely balance of size and distance needed to make the moon look just big enough to cover the sun, the unlikely way in which the Earth acquired the moon, the fact that eclipses will only be seen in our time); or, two, it's God saying hello.

Removing my tongue from my cheek, I'd like to argue that the latter explanation should not be dismissed too hastily. I submit that any Supreme Being would be sorely tempted to sign His/Her work, since He/She would probably have a supreme ego, or at least a supreme sense of humor. He/She would want to take credit for the work. And how would He/She do this? There are lots of ways. He/She could be really sneaky and hide His/Her signature as the supreme beings did in the book Contact, by Carl Sagan (not the movie).

In the book, the protagonist, Ellie Arroway, discovers a signal from space that turns out to be instructions for building a machine. The machine, as luck would have it, is some sort of transporter, and our heroine is swept away to unknown shores where she meets her long-deceased father, who is really an alien who has read her mind. He tells her that his people did not create the wormhole rapid transit system that swept her away. Rather, those super-advanced entities left; they went somewhere. But proof that they exist could be found in pi (π). When she gets home, no one believes her story, and she is ostracized. She decides to prove her story by looking into pi, so she goes to a big computer and has it print out pi to more decimal places than have ever been calculated before. She finds that at the nth decimal place the integers of pi start turning up 1s and 0s instead of the random numbers that pi is famous for. The 1s and 0s form a code, and when she breaks the code, the message comes out to be a perfect circle. In this story, the entities who created the universe (and, with it, pi) could not resist putting a clue in the number pi that the universe was created by an intelligent force, that it was not accidental or random. In other words, they couldn't resist signing their work.

That, I think, is what eclipses are. At least they would be if I were God. Perhaps that is why they bring tears to my eyes.

Sarsens

*a*s I crested the rise that looked down upon the monument, I felt an involuntary catch in my breath. The stones were illuminated by the reds and golds of sunset, a lighting that no West-End professional could hope to match. The giant Sarsens cast long umbrae toward the east as the sun dropped silently yet dramatically into the occidental sky. And as the last piece of Lucifer's progeny disappeared below the western margin, a new brilliance took its place, only this time appearing at the sun's antipode. It was the Blood Moon, and it was rising over what was to become the greatest adventure of my life.

In the fall of 1989, I was teaching for the semester in London. I had arrived two months early because I was interested in exploring the beginning of science—the philosophy that makes the modern world go, the method of inquiry that allows us to put planes in the air, men on the moon, tomatoes on our winter tables, vaccines in our hypodermics, Teflon valves in our hearts, cell phones in our pockets and tigers in our tanks.

Where did science begin? I thought that I might find the answer in the rich scientific tradition of the British Isles, a tradition that stretches back, down the corridors of time; before Cavendish, Maxwell, and Thomson, physicists of the Nineteenth and early Twentieth Centuries; before Newton, Halley and Hooke, astronomers and physicists of the Renaissance; perhaps back thousands of years to the builders of the standing stone monuments, which, it is claimed by some, are instruments of astronomical science—computers for the prediction of celestial events.

If these claims are true, if a 5,000-year-old, standing-stone monument is truly an astronomical computer capable of predicting events as complex as solar eclipses, then perhaps we were wrong in placing the dawn of scientific inquiry at the doorstep of the Greeks of 500-1000 BCE, who flourished in the backwaters of the mighty Aegean. Could it be that science goes back twice that far—not 2,500 years but, rather, 5,000 years? I didn't know how I was going to answer the question, but I was convinced that the standing stones held the key. They were, in a sense, the repository of my Holy Grail.

I decided to start at the top, so to speak, with, possibly the oldest and surely the most famous standing stones, the 5,000-year-old standing stones at Sarum, otherwise known as Stonehenge. Stonehenge is an impossibly massive and complex circle of erect and fallen blocks of sandstone, some crested with lintels, most weighing twenty-five to forty-five tons, which until modern times was considered to be a monument of purely religious or ritualistic significance. However, in the last few decades, owing largely to the work of Boston University's Gerald Hawkins, it has been seen as an astronomical observatory—an ancient computer for the prediction of celestial phenomena, chief of which was the direction of the rising mid-summer sun, but also including events as complex as solar eclipses, events that today are predictable only with the aid of high-speed computers.

My first attempt to visit Stonehenge came in mid-July, at the height of the tourist season. The result was entirely disappointing; the monument was overrun with people, creating a circus-like atmosphere that made any communion with the stones impossible. Moreover, the entire monument was cordoned off, protected by a rope to keep the hoards at bay. While this did indeed protect the stones, it resulted in isolating the visitor from the full impact of the monument. I left Stonehenge disappointed and dejected. The whole affair felt unfinished.

As it happened, Rob Bryson, a friend of mine from a neighboring college, was representing our consortium in London that semester. Rob was an instructor of photography. I had met Rob years before at a photography conference, at which he had presented a paper on full moon photography. The idea was to visit some famous site on the night of a full moon and use this moonlight for the photograph. At the conference, Rob had shown several of the places he had visited, as well as the full-moon-illuminated subject. His methodology was interesting and his results beautiful.

I had all but forgotten Rob's hobby when one October day, while sitting in a London pub eating lunch between classes, he looked over at me and said, "By the way, I wrote to the minister in charge of antiquities and got permission to photograph Stonehenge at the next full moon. Want to come along for the ride? You can drive." I looked at him in disbelief.

"Who else will be there?" I asked.

"Just the two of us," he replied

"What about the rope?"

"Oh, it'll be down for the photography."

"How long can we stay?"

"From sunset to sunrise, more than twelve hours."

"I can't believe it," I said. "How'd ya' pull it off?"

"Oh," he replied with a wink. "Just native charm."

I couldn't believe my good fortune. For the second time, I headed west out of London and toward the Salisbury Plains. As we drove into the setting sun, I felt a tug from the west, as if the sun were urging me forward toward the resolution of my quest. Both Rob and I were charged, but for different reasons. He knew what he wanted from Stonehenge, and he knew how to get it. I had only a vague idea as to what I wanted, and I had absolutely no idea how to get it.

It was just before sunset when I steered the car into the completely-deserted parking lot. We parked and scurried up the path toward the monument. We checked in at the low-slung, flat-roofed guardhouse to let them know we were there and continued up the path. I could see the lunar orb just peeking over the eastern horizon, its bloated form and sanguine hue giving mute testimony to its appellation, Blood Moon. I noted wryly that the phenomenon I was observing juxtaposed the diagonal opposites of the success of science at wresting nature's secrets from her iron grip: the color of the low-altitude full moon and its swollen appearance. To the first phenomenon, science has the answers securely in hand. The red-orange of the rising full moon is due the propensity of the Earth's atmosphere to scatter the blue light from the incoming moonbeam, leaving just the reds to enter the eye.

However, science has not yet explained the second phenomenon, the apparently bloated moon. We know that this phenomenon is an illusion, that the moon is really no bigger when it is on the horizon than at any other time. We've known about this phenomenon for thousands of years, and we're little closer to explaining it than we were at the time of the ancient Greeks. The point is that there are natural phenomena that we have explained and phenomena that we have not explained. Most importantly, we freely admit it. This intellectual honesty is a basic tenet of science. It is not a sin to be ignorant. The sin is in the false claim of understanding when there is no understanding at hand. In this way, science differs from other fields of human endeavor, such as politics, or religion. In these more subjective areas, answers are made up all the time, with little regard for objective truth. For an explanation of what happened at Stonehenge 4,000 to 5,000 years ago to be science, it would have to conform to the standard of intellectual honesty, among others.

Rob and I crested the rise that looked down upon the monument. There it was! We were in awe—transfixed. We stopped dead in our tracks and just stood for I don't know how long. Then, silently and slowly, we walked the rest of the way down the path, across about thirty meters of luxuriant, newly-mown grass, to the nearest upright in the Sarsen Circle. I put my hands on the stone, feeling its smooth surface polished by the weather of centuries. I sniffed its musky dampness and tasted its sweetness.

I stretched out my mind, searching for the past, trying to connect with the history of the place. I stroked, sniffed, tasted and stretched for maybe five to ten minutes, and all I got for my efforts was a feel, a smell, a taste and nothing else. Then it hit me and I started laughing. What an idiot I had been. How could it have been any other way? How could I possibly have expected to get anything more from the place than what I got from my five senses? What had I expected to happen? Did I expect a big booming voice from the sky to shout out the answers to my questions? It was absurd. I had come here pretending to be a scientist, with questions about the origin of science, and I had expected the answers to come from . . . where? The sky? The ground? Maybe the stones themselves? Whatever I had expected, it wasn't science.

I knew what science was. Science was archeology. Science was anthropology. Science was radiometric dating. But these fields of study had spoken and because they did not have the answers that I was looking for, I had come here hoping for—yes, that's right—magic!

"What's so funny, Max?" called Rob. He had walked inside the Trilithon Horseshoe and was standing next to the Altar Stone.

"Oh, it was nothing," I said, turning and walking toward him. "I'll tell you later," I continued, resolving not to tell him later.

Later it is," he repeated. "Want to help with the photography? It'll go faster that way and it's getting cold out here."

Rob was right. With the sun out of the sky, the temperature was dropping rapidly, and it was only mid-October. I'd hate to be out here in the middle of the night at mid-winter, I thought to myself.

"Sure," I answered. "Whadayah want me to do?"

"You can paint while I take the pictures."

"Paint?" I said, puzzled.

"Yeah," he said. "I'll man the camera during the time exposures, and you will run around with the strobe, illuminating the stones. But you have to keep moving. If you stop, the camera will pick up your image, and you'll be in the picture."

"O.K." I said.

"Let's do it!" he said.

We spent the next three hours photographing the stones. Rob manned the camera while I ran around with the strobe following his instructions. I firmly understood the process and principles he was using, but I had no sense of the exposure times and f/stops. For this work, practical experience was everything.

Finally we were finished. "I'm freezing," I said. "How much longer are we going to be out here?"

"We're almost done," Rob replied. "Only one thing left to do."

"What's that?" I said, hoping it would be very short. The cold was getting painful.

"Get a souvenir," he replied smiling broadly. "Go sit on the Altar Stone, facing the moon."

"OK," I said, as I turned and strode off in the direction of the large fallen stone, which seemed to be at the focus of all of the other stones. Rob walked off and stationed himself about fifty feet from me, directly between the moon and where I was sitting. While he set up the tripod and camera, he gave me instructions.

In two minutes he was done. "Now I'll do me and we'll be outa here."

"What can I do?" I asked.

"Nothing," he replied. "I can do it myself. Just relax for a few minutes."

I nodded in his direction and leaned back until my head was resting on the stone. I was completely supine, except for my feet, which dangled over the side of the rock. I thought of the twists and turns in my life that had conspired to bring me to this place and time, the events that necessarily occurred to make my world line intersect with that of Stonehenge. It was all too weird. Through half-closed eyes, I saw the giant stones . . . Rob exposing his own picture, posing in front of one of the Trilithons . . . the brilliant full moon illuminating the whole unlikely event. There, just above the nearest Trilithon where Rob was standing was Polaris, the North Star, marker for the

North Celestial Pole and the current direction of the axis of rotation of our magnificent and entirely ordinary planet. Near Polaris stood the Big Dipper, which at this place and time was just completing lower culmination, its handle pointing toward the northern horizon, its bowl in an orientation that would make it difficult to hold water.

I looked over at Rob again. He was still working. Boy, I thought, what a great hobby he has, running around the world photographing its wonders. Where was he going next? My memory strained to remember what he had told me. Oh, yeah, Kilamanjaro. Wow!'

It had been a long day and fatigue was catching up with me. I decided to close my eyes for a few moments. Since Rob would be rousting me up in a few minutes, there was little chance of freezing to death. Anyway, I thought, what better place to die than on the Altar Stone at Stonehenge?

A hot breeze wafted by my cheek. The warmth felt good after the hours of cold. That's odd, I mused, slightly disoriented. This warmth was really sudden and unseasonable. I half opened my eyes and was greeted by . . . nothing.

It was almost completely dark, the only light coming from the stars. I'd seen dark, starry nights before, and this one seemed no different. But in some strange disquieting way, it was different. For a moment I couldn't put my finger on it. Then I remembered. There was no moon. A few minutes ago, the moon had been full. Now it was gone. My mind searched for an explanation, some foundation upon which to place my feet.

"I'm dreaming," I said to the Altar Stone.

"No you're not," said the stone. "You know what dreams feel like. Does this feel like that?"

"No, it doesn't," I replied.

"And you know what reality feels like. Does this feel like that?

"Well . . . yes," I admitted. "But where's the moon?"

"Maybe it set," interjected my scientist-side.

"No good," I shot back, unease bordering on fear. "You know better than that. It was a full moon, and a full moon rises at sunset and sets at sunrise. If it had set, the sun would be up, and it would be daytime." Disorientation and fear begot dizziness and nausea.

Then I remembered Rob. I called out his name. No reply. I reached into my pocket. A small amount of relief washed over me as my hand felt the familiar curved shaft of my mag-light. At least that much reality remained. I pulled out the light, pointed it in the direction where Rob was when I last saw him, and punched the rubberized, waterproof button. At the speed of light I felt relief. There was Rob, sitting, obviously sleeping, leaning up against the base of the nearest Trilithon. I called his name again, louder this time. He stirred and opened his eyes.

"OK, Max" he murmured sleepily. "I'm ready to go."

"Just a minute," I croaked, trying to quell the tremor I felt creeping into my voice. "Come over here!"

"What?" he said, not yet fully released from sleep.

"Come over here, please!"

"OK. OK." Rob climbed to his feet and walked toward my flashlight, shielding his eyes with his hand so he could see the ground in front of him.

"What's the matter?" he said as he reached the Altar Stone.

"Does anything seem strange to you?" I asked, hoping that he could make some sense of this for me.

"Strange? Nooooo," he replied slowly. "It's gotten kinda warm."

"Kinda warm? It must have warmed up fifty degrees! And what about the moon?"

"What about the moon?" he repeated, tilting his head upward and scanning the sky. After about half a minute, he turned his head back in my direction. "I guess it set while we were dozing," he said, hesitantly.

"No." I said. "That's not possible. The full moon sets at sunrise. If it had set, it would be daytime now."

"I know that," said Rob, his tone somewhere between confused and insulted. He looked up at the sky again, searching for something that would provide a simple explanation to the puzzle. After what seemed like an eternity but what only was about fifteen seconds, he gave up. "Wow," he hissed, sinking down to sit unsteadily on the Altar Stone beside me.

"That's right, 'Wow.'"

"Could this be a dream?" he looked at me hopefully.

"What do you think?" I asked. "Do you think that you're dreaming this?"

"Well, if it is a dream, it's like no dream I've ever had."

"Besides, if it is a dream, which one of us is doing the dreaming? We both can't be dreaming the same dream, or can we? This is really weird."

"We should go back to the car and see if it's OK," Rob said, weakly.

"OK," I replied, but as I headed off to the path to the parking lot, Rob did not move. He just stood there staring toward the east.

"I don't remember a big city out there," he mused, almost to himself.

I turned and looked. Sure enough, the southeastern horizon was aglow. "No," I confirmed, "that light was not there before. And why do you think it's a city?"

"Well, what else could it be," he countered.

"I don't know," I said. Then, trying to be clever, "Maybe it's the sunrise."

"Sunrise!" he fairly shouted. "The sun went down not four hours ago, and the nights in the winter here are fifteen or sixteen hours long. We weren't sleeping that long."

"Well, if it is sunrise, we'll know soon enough," I said, resignedly.

We sat down on the Altar Stone, waiting to see what would happen. A vague curiosity nudged away our fear. We forgot about the car as we mimicked the stone on which we sat, waiting for . . . something.

After about two minutes, Rob said, "I think it's getting brighter."

"It certainly is," I concurred. "The sunrise hypothesis takes the lead."

Rob didn't bother commenting. He was studying the southeast, watching the illumination on the horizon, which was now becoming very bright. We both realized what we were watching at the same time. "It's the moon," we said in unison.

"It can't be but . . ."

". . . but it has to be." Rob finished my sentence.

At that moment, the limb of the moon broke above the horizon. I was almost, but not quite, speechless. It wasn't the limb, the curved natural edge of the moon I was seeing. It was the terminator, the boundary between lunar day and lunar night. What's more, it was perfectly straight, the hallmark of the quarter moon. The fact that the western half of the moon was dark, while the eastern half was illuminated, told me that it was a last quarter moon, the phase that occurs seven days after full.

We sat in stunned silence for the ten minutes it took the last quarter moon to come fully above the horizon.

I looked at my watch. "Well, at least we know that our watches are right. The last quarter moon rises at midnight."

Rob looked at his watch. "Yup, it's midnight by my watch."

"So," I said, "We know what time of the day it is, but we don't know what day of the week it is. We came out here on a full moon, and six hours later we have a last quarter moon."

"Am I supposed to believe that seven days have passed in the last six hours?"

"No," I said thoughtfully. "We don't have enough data to draw any conclusions. For example, we don't know how many lunations have occurred since we arrived."

"What's a lunation?" asked Rob.

"Oh, sorry," I replied. "A lunation is the period of revolution of the moon, about thirty days. So we may have arrived seven days ago or thirty-seven or sixty-seven or 30,007. How can we tell? In fact, it's possible that it's now twenty-three days before we arrived or fifty-three days or eighty-three days. We can't rule anything out. Wait, I have an idea." I looked up into the northern sky to see the position of the Big Dipper. When I had last looked, about an hour ago, the handle had been pointing towards the ground. Now, the Dipper was totally upside down with the handle pointing east.

"Look," I said. "Let's say, for the sake of argument, that it's midnight. The rising last quarter moon is a pretty good argument for that assumption. Now, look at the Big Dipper.

It's upside down. So, when is the Dipper upside down at midnight?"

"How should I know," Rob said. "You're the astronomer."

"Right you are. Sorry again," I said. "The Dipper is upside down at midnight in late June. Just about at the summer solstice."

"You're not trying to tell me that we came out here in the middle of October and now, just a few hours later, it's late June. That's nuts!"

"I'm not trying to tell you anything," I said, sounding a little defensive. "That conclusion is based on the simplest of observations taken at face value. There's no reason to question the data and the data lead to a simple conclusion. There's only one reason to question the conclusion . . . it's nuts. But we have no objective evidence that it's not true, and we have other circumstantial evidence that it is."

"What's that," Rob asked.

"The temperature," I said, almost beginning to believe the conclusion myself. "Is this temperature consistent with a night in late October or a night in late June?"

"June," he grudgingly admitted.

"Right," I continued. I was on a roll, and I wanted to become immersed in it. I didn't want to think about how crazy the situation was or the consequences if it were true. So for the sake of my sanity, I took on the mantle of pure scientist.

"So, what do we have?" I said. "We agree that we arrived here on October 18th at about sunset, and now the sky tells us that it's late June, but which June we don't know. Do you agree with all that?"

"Yes, I guess so," Rob said unhappily and in a whisper, as though saying it aloud would make it true.

"OK. You watch the moon. Do you remember its phase around the last summer solstice?" I asked.

"No, but I think I can reconstruct it," he said, brightening a bit. "I remember that I went to Devil's Postpile on the June full moon to photograph it. And I also remember that I was unhappy because it occurred four days short of the solstice. I always note synchronous celestial events. I like them. I don't know why."

"Everyone likes them," I added. "It makes you feel that there's some symmetry in the universe, some rhyme or reason. A totally capricious universe is scary."

"I guess so."

"So, you're saying that the moon was a waning gibbous at the last summer solstice," I confirmed.

"Yup!"

"Well, that's close to what we have now—three or four days off what we have now. It could be evidence that this, tonight, is near the June 1989 solstice, but I don't think it's strong enough evidence. I still don't think we know what year it is."

"Listen to yourself!" yelled Rob. "You're really getting into this. I think you're enjoying it."

"Well," I said, examining my motives, "it is what's happening. Would we be better off if we denied it . . . or sat on the rock wringing our hands?"

"I don't know," Rob replied. "Maybe, if this is a dream or an hallucination, we would be better off fighting it than assuming it's reality."

"I'll tell you what," I said, smile invisible in the darkness, "you fight it, I'll go with it, and we'll see who gets home first."

"I know who'll get home first," laughed Rob.

"Who?" I asked.

"The one who finds the car first."

"Speaking of the car," I said, standing up. "We were going to check it out. I think we should do that." Although I didn't verbalize it, I was wondering what we would do if the car were not there. I pushed the thought out of my mind. It was too scary.

I started walking toward the path that led to the parking lot. Rob followed, lugging the equipment, lagging two or three steps behind. "The car has to be there," he said. "I just can't imagine this getting any worse."

At that moment, Rob ran into me from behind. "Whoops," he gasped, ramming me with the tripod. "Sorry about that. Are you OK?"

Stopped dead in my tracks, I was looking forward and upward, at an angle of about twenty-five degrees to the horizontal. I neither felt the impact nor heard his question. "Things just got worse," I heard myself say. "Much, much worse!"

"You're kidding," said Rob, half-declaring and half-questioning as he followed my gaze into the heavens. "What do you see?"

"Look at Polaris!" I commanded, trying to keep the fear, which had returned, out of my voice.

"Yeah, I see it. So what?

"Well, you know that Polaris marks the position of the north celestial pole. And the position of the pole relative to the horizon is the same as your latitude. When we got here Polaris was in its proper place. About fifty degrees up. But now, its altitude is about half that. The pole star is not supposed to move over short times."

"What does that mean?" asked Rob, hesitantly. It was obvious that he really didn't want to hear my answer.

"Well, off the top of my head, I can think of two possibilities for that sort of displacement. One is that we've been moved southward by . . . let's see . . . one degree is sixty nautical miles, so we have twenty-five degrees of shift times sixty nautical miles per degree. That would be about . . . ummmm . . . 1,500 nautical miles!"

"That's crazy," said Rob. "I still think we're dreaming."

"I admit that the dream hypothesis is the most comforting," I submitted, "but that in itself is no reason to believe it. I can see no evidence for that explanation. Without evidence, that explanation is no better than religion. You might just as well blame God."

"I disagree," interjected Rob. "We know that dreams exist while we don't know that God does. So I think that it's more likely that our current situation is due to dreaming than it is to God."

"Maybe so," I conceded. "I'll have to think about it later. But I think we can safely say for now that, if we're in a dream, it will take care of itself. We don't have to do anything about it—in fact, we really can't do anything about it. But if it's not a dream—in other words, if this is real—we may have the power to act. In fact, we may have to act to protect ourselves. So I think it's best to assume the worst. Then, if we're wrong, we'll be better off than we thought we'd be.

"So, I told you that I had an explanation other than that we've been displaced southward by about 1,500 miles. If this hypothesis is true, that is, if we can dig up sufficient evidence for it, it's the worst possible situation for us, so it's best to get it out in the open so we can deal with it."

"OK, shoot," replied Rob.

"Well," I said, "on what can we agree?"

"That we're probably dreaming?"

"No!" I said. "Cut that out!"

"OK, OK. That it's not when we think it should be," said Rob resignedly.

"Yes," I continued, "the evidence from the phase of the moon and the position of the stars is that we're some time other than the time we think it should be, namely about midnight on the night of October 16/17, 1989. But exactly when it is we don't know except that it's at least a week from when we thought it should be. So, we know that we have a problem with time. On the other hand, we don't know that we have a problem with space. In fact, there is evidence that we don't have a problem with space."

"What is that?"

"It's just this," I said. "We came to Stonehenge; we fell asleep at Stonehenge; we awoke at Stonehenge and we're still at Stonehenge. The change in altitude of Polaris is the only evidence for a change in location, and there's another way to explain that."

"OK," he said, "I'm all attention. What is it?"

"Simple," I said. "Precession. The north celestial pole precesses, or wobbles, in a slow circle that takes 26,000 years to complete."

"So," Rob said, "you're suggesting that the Earth's wobble has shifted the north celestial pole away from Polaris so that the altitude of Polaris no longer represents our latitude."

"Could be," I concurred.

"If you're right, then, if we can find the pole, its position relative to Polaris will tell us how far in time we are from the time when the pole pointed toward Polaris, which is, of course, around 2000 AD."

"Yes," I said. "We know that 5,000 years ago, in 3,000 BCE the pole star was Thuban. We just find the pole now and, depending on where it is, either extrapolate or interpolate from Thuban and Polaris."

"Right," said Rob, excitedly. "How should we begin?"

"Well," I said, nervousness being replaced by academic curiosity, "I think we should start at the Altar Stone." I stood up and walked over to the mammoth horizontal piece of sandstone, which was the focus of the entire monument and upon which I had taken the nap that to all appearances had catapulted Rob and me somewhere else in time.

"Just before I fell asleep on this stone I saw Polaris just above that Trilithon. As a first try, I believe the north celestial pole is still there, about fifty degrees in altitude, but the sky has shifted relative to the pole due to precession. So, all we have to do is look for the center of the diurnal circles of the stars and—bingo—we'll have it. Then we'll compare the present north celestial pole to Thuban and Polaris and we'll have an estimate of when we are."

"Let's do it," said Rob.

We sat on the Altar Stone and using the Trilithon as a reference we searched for that one point in the sky that did not move, the hallmark of a celestial pole. It was a difficult task, for the sky moves very slowly and there was no guarantee that the north celestial pole would be near a bright star. But after about two hours of observing, we thought we had the right place, a blank place in the sky, just about halfway between Polaris and Thuban.

"Well, that's it," I said. "The stars above that point are moving to the left and below that point to the right. The stars to the left are moving down and the stars to the right are moving up. In my book that defines the celestial pole."

"And," Rob continued, "since the pole appears to be halfway between Polaris and Thuban, we must be at a time halfway between 2000 AD and 3000 BCE. That puts us at 500 BCE. And if you believe that, I've got a bridge in Arizona."

"You have to believe it," I replied. "All the observations fit, and there is no evidence for any other hypothesis."

"I still vote for dreaming," Rob said. "Nothing else makes sense."

"Maybe so," I replied, "but remember, we decided to treat this situation as real so that if we had to act, we would be prepared."

"OK, so we're making believe it's 500 BCE," sighed Rob.

"No, we're assuming it is 500 BCE," I corrected.

"All right, all right. What now?" Rob said with syrupy resignation in his voice.

"I haven't the slightest idea," I said softly. I had run out of ideas. "What time is it anyway?" I asked hoping to change the subject—as though that were possible.

Rob glanced at the sky, ignoring his watch, which he probably didn't trust. "The moon's just a little more than halfway to the meridian, so it must be between 3:00 and 4:00 a.m."

I was getting very tired. We needed a plan that seemed like action but really wasn't. "If this is really late June," I said, "the sun should be coming up soon. The safest thing would be to wait until it's light. It might be easier to sort things out then."

Yeah," agreed Rob, also glad for the opportunity to continue sitting. "And maybe the guards will come," he added as an afterthought.

"Yes," I echoed, hopefully. "Maybe the guards will come."

We walked over to the Altar Stone, sat down and waited for the sun. As we sat, we chatted, noting that our spirits were rising. Rob started singing and was in the middle of his somewhat skewed version of "Here Comes the Sun" when he stopped in mid-sentence.

"What the hell is that?" he queried, craning his neck to peek around a nearby standing stone.

"Where?" I responded, turning to look back over my shoulder, in the direction of his gaze. There, low on the horizon several miles distant was a series of lights, a procession of lights, although I could not tell immediately if they were moving.

"What the devil is that?" I said, half under my breath, half to no one in particular. We sat in silence for a few minutes, watching. Finally, Rob said, "I think they're moving . . . and I think they're moving this way."

"Are you sure?" I asked, feeling for the nth time a slight anxiety rising.

"No, I'm not sure yet. Let's wait a little longer before we do anything."

"Do anything?" I repeated. "What do you suggest we do?"

"I don't know. Run . . . hide?"

"Maybe it's the guards," I said, hopefully.

"Yeah, right," said Rob, the facetiousness evident in his voice. "It's the guards, a hundred of them, all carrying torches, and dressed in white robes."

"Really?" I asked, unsure about whether he was kidding me. I turned to look at him and found him looking through a small pair of binoculars, which he had produced from his jacket pocket. He obviously took my question as rhetorical as he silently scanned the horizon.

After about a minute he lowered his field glasses and looked at me squarely. "They are coming this way," he announced solemnly. "What should we do?"

"I know what I'm going to do," I said, excitedly. "I'm going to get to the bottom of this. I'm going to find out exactly where and when we are."

"And how do you propose to do this?" inquired Rob.

"Simple. I'll ask them," was my reply.

"Not so fast," Rob cautioned. "Let's think about this for a second before we do something we'll be sorry for."

"Sorry for? Why?" I asked.

"Because, if we were right in our reasoning—and although I don't like the thought of it, I'm beginning to think we might have been—we don't know anything about these people. Do they speak English? Will they appreciate strangers? Maybe they are violent. After all, there have been stories of sacrifices, human sacrifices, carried out here. And even if we were wrong about being thrown into the past, we'll still be uninvited guests crashing somebody's party. They may not like it, and there are a lot of them. So I say, in this case, discretion is the better part of valor."

"OK, that's wise," I said, calming down. "What should we do then?"

"We can back off some, a few hundred feet maybe, and watch from a distance."

"Or we could hide behind one of the stones in the Circle. We'd be a lot closer and more hidden," I said.

"That wouldn't work," Rob interjected. "There are so many of them that they'll fill the entire monument. There would be no place to hide from them. We have to get away from the Circle."

"But it's so bright out there that we'll be seen unless we're behind something. I've got it! Let's hide behind the Heel Stone. We'll be far from the Circle and behind something. The best of all possible worlds."

"Nice work, Pangloss. Let's do it."

We walked toward the Heel Stone, which was about a hundred feet from the Sarsen Circle. When we reached it, we took a position behind it and waited. The procession slowly approached us. After about ten minutes, they were only a few hundred yards away.

"They're moving pretty quietly," Rob whispered to me.

I suddenly realized that he was right. A group that size should make some sound with their feet, even if no one was talking. This group was absolutely silent—not one sound. It was impossible. Still they continued to come. As the leaders of the procession passed the front of the Trilithon, I felt myself grow weak. I couldn't believe what I was seeing.

"Do you see what I see?" I asked Rob, in a hoarse whisper.

"I see it, but I don't believe it," said Rob weakly. "Now I know I'm dreaming."

There in front of us, counter to everything we thought was possible, were men passing through a Trilithon Arch, and as they did so, the rocks could be seen through their bodies. They were transparent, like a double exposure. Not one of Rob's planned double exposures—that looks right, with each exposure retaining its own solidity—but a double exposure gone awry, one body embedded grotesquely into the other.

We watched in disbelief as they came. Ethereal figure after ethereal figure cloaked in long white robes, gliding, single-file, smoothly and silently over the rugged and boulder-strewn landscape. One by one they entered the Sarsen Circle, making a right angle turn as they crossed inside and walking along its circumference until they were as the Sarsens, arrayed in a circle of slightly smaller diameter. And still they came. Only now they were creating a larger circle of men (at least it looked like they were all men) about twice the diameter of the Sarsen Circle.

Finally they finished coming. And they just stood there . . . and stood there . . . and stood there. About one hundred men divided in half and forming two circles, one just inside the Sarsen Circle and one about twice that diameter . . . just standing there.

It was unnerving. From the very beginning we had no sound. Now we had no motion. The scene had tuned into a snapshot. We seemed to be losing dimension after dimension. Would the whole scene disappear soon? Would it fade to black, after which I would open my eyes to find that it had, after all, been only a dream? As I watched with fascination, my psyche engaged in a titanic tug of war. On one side of the rope, the fearful me was praying that it would be a dream, that I would wake up and find that all of the events of the last few hours had been just an hallucination—an unimaginably realistic hallucination but an hallucination nevertheless. Hell, I'd even throw in the trip to Stonehenge with Rob for the sake of sanity. Let that be a part of the hallucination, too. Anything, just get me outta here!

But, fortunately, there was the braver, more curious me on the other side of the rope. The me that was not incapacitated by the possible danger inherent in this situation. The me that wanted to know what was going on and would not rest until he did. That was the me that I need to tap into at this moment, the me that would keep my body from running off into the night.

Holding on to the Heel Stone to stabilize myself, I watched in silence. After what seemed like an eternity but was probably no more than five minutes, a figure broke from the ranks of the inner circle and moved, or floated, to the outer circle. There, he reached into his tunic and pulled out some object or set of objects and started manipulating them. Because his back was partially turned toward us, I could see neither what he held nor what he was doing. I can only assume that it was some sort of device for making fire, iron and flint, for example, because after a few moments I saw a flame develop in his palm and burn steadily. Then he proceeded to walk around the inside of the outer circle of men, stopping and lighting some material at the feet of each man. When he was finished, the outer circle had become a ring of fire, half a hundred burning with a steady light. Then, for the second time that day—déjà vu. I had seen such a circle before. But where?

Then I had it! The Aubrey holes! Those fires marked the positions of the fifty-six modern day Aubrey holes, excavated pits discovered by John Aubrey in the 17th Century, some refilled with chalk, whose purpose have remained an enigma to modern archeologists. Was that mystery about to be solved?

Then, while the man with the master flame retreated to the inner circle, each person making up the outer circle reached inside his tunic and pulled out a small object. Given our distance and the dim lighting, it was impossible to tell exactly what the object was but, and I'm not sure about this, it seemed as though some of these objects might be moving.

If what I was thinking was correct, there were going to be fifty-six dead somethings out there real soon. What should I do? What *could* I do? Not only were we vastly outnumbered, but I also didn't know whether our world lines had actually intersected, whether I was actually at the same time and place as these people. The way it looked to me, there may have been partial or pseudo-intersection occurring, one in which certain dimensions intersect while others do not. In such a case interaction would be seriously compromised or impossible. All I could do was watch what happened next.

No sound initiated the next action. No one on either circle gave a signal or sign. Simultaneously, all of the men in the outer circle dropped to their knees, their hands held high over their heads cupping the objects that I assumed were alive. In front of each of them was a burning Aubrey hole. In unison they brought their arms down and threw the objects into the fire. In my imagination, I could hear the screams of the small animals that I assumed had just been put to death. But, of course, there was no sound to be heard from the mute ritual in front of us.

At this point, three figures broke from the inner circle and walked to its center where the Altar Stone that I had slept on sat. At the same time, two people from the opposite side of the inner circle broke ranks and moved towards the center. It was immediately obvious that one of these two figures was different from the rest. This figure had the obvious form of a young female.

My heart almost stopped. Were we about to witness a human sacrifice? All of the uncertainty, disorientation and fear surrounding what had transpired over the past few hours paled at the thought of what might happen next.

"What should we do?" I hissed to Rob.

"What can we do?" came the reply.

I fell silent. Indeed, what could we do? The answer was pretty straightforward. Nothing! Nothing at all! Again, all we could do was watch.

The young girl was led to the Altar Stone where she, with no hint of resistance, first sat, and then leaned back to put herself in a supine position, much as I had done just a few hours before. The three men who had walked from the inner circle to the Altar Stone now surrounded the stone, standing at the vertices of an imaginary equilateral triangle. One of the men was at her feet while the other two stood at her arms. The two men at her sides sank to their knees, hands together in front of them in what one would call a praying position. The figure at her feet raised his arms above his head, hands together, in a manner that one would consider threatening—if he had had a weapon. But I could see no weapon. His hands, at least from this distance, appeared empty. He was threatening her with . . . nothing.

Then I noticed that the people who made up the outer circle had started circling, moving laterally counterclockwise, from Aubrey hole to Aubrey hole, at the same time holding their hands and arms in the classic position of prayer.

I turned back to the central attraction, to the Altar Stone at the focus of the Trilithon horseshoe, just in time to see the figure with upraised arms bring them down rapidly in a thrusting motion, which would have been deadly to the young girl if his hands had held a weapon. Then the two men, who seemed to be praying, got up and gently helped the young woman to her feet, and, together, the three of them walked back and melted into the circle from which they had come.

"Well," I whispered to Rob, "whatever else these people are, they're not murderers. At least not of humans. That was a ritual sacrifice."

"I'm not convinced they're safe," Rob replied, barely audible. "Let's be careful—*and quiet.*"

I nodded in agreement and turned back to the ritual taking place among the stones. Now, something new was happening. The outer circle was beginning to dissolve. One person at a time, consecutively, left the circle and walked in a line, down the Avenue, toward the Heel Stone . . . *toward us!*

"Oh God, they're coming this way," hissed Rob through clenched teeth.

"Hang on. Hang on. They may not be able to hear or see us," I said, hoping against hope that my wishful thinking was actually intuition. The first walker was now heading straight for us, ten yards distant. With only the Heel Stone between us and our hearts threatening to jump out of our mouths, the man walked just to the left of the stone and continued walking in a straight line, down the Avenue, away from the Sarsens. Now he was on our side of the Heel Stone, and we were in plain sight! Yet he showed no sign that he saw us. No surprise. No hesitation. No recognition of anything unusual. He walked silently past us and continued radially, walking away from both the Heel Stone and the Sarsens. Immediately he was followed by the second walker, and the third, and the fourth, and the fifth. In all, about thirty men passed our position, heading linearly along the Avenue and into the night. None of them gave any sign that they saw us. Somehow, we, despite lacking the dimension of sound from their world, were receiving more information about them than they were about us. It was, I guessed, some artifact of the spacetime continuum that I did not understand. But, given everything that had happened to us this evening, I was in no position to be surprised.

All of a sudden, they stopped walking.

"What the hell are they doing?" I said to no one in particular. They had constructed, out of men, a human chain that extended from the Altar Stone at the center of the Henge out to the Heel Stone and beyond, about three hundred feet. In unison they pulled from their tunics a long cylindrical object, about the size and shape of a relay baton, which they held high over their heads pointing toward the zenith.

Again, the flamemaster separated from the inner circle and walked radially down the Avenue, stopping at each man in the chain to transfer fire from his source to what now was obviously a torch. When he was finished, we were left with a blazing line of light, about five hundred feet long, extending like an arrow down the Avenue, from the Altar Stone, past the Heel Stone, and beyond.

As I looked down the line of torches from my position behind the Heel Stone, I noticed, for the second time that evening, a glow in the east. This time, however, it was in the northeast rather that the southeast. I studied the glow, conjuring a likely hypothesis. It couldn't be the moon, for the moon, having risen about six hours ago, was already high in the sky and approaching the meridian. What might it be?

"Hey Rob," I whispered loudly. "What is that light in the northeast?"

Rob gazed toward the northeast horizon and then up at the moon. "Are you kidding?" he asked.

"No," I replied, beginning to realize that I had asked a stupid question before I even knew it.

"Look at the moon!" he almost shouted. "That, my astronomer friend," he said, pointing to the glow on the horizon that I had been puzzling over, "is the sunrise!"

Even before he even finished his sentence, I knew he was right. I knew that the last quarter moon crosses the meridian at sunrise as well as I knew anything. It was just that the events of the last twelve hours had been so disorienting that I didn't know if I really knew anything, any more.

Then, like the slow motion film of an explosion viewed in reverse, all the pieces of the whole, starting from margins of the vista, slowly came into view, drawing toward the center of the field, there reassembling themselves to make the whole once more.

It would take the sunrise to prove I was correct—that and one, possibly foolish, act. Slowly yet deliberately I moved from my position of relative security out from behind the Heel Stone and into the open. In front of me was the monument: the Sarsen Circle, the mighty Trilithon horseshoe, about eighty people, or pseudopeople and, the focus of all of the geometry and interest, the Altar Stone. Behind me was the Heel Stone. And stretching from the Altar Stone to the Heel Stone and beyond was a line of men, yards apart, each facing northeast, along the direction of the line, each holding a flaming torch—the infinitude of one-dimension points that defines a line.

I started moving forward, toward the Altar Stone and along the line of torch-bearing men. From behind me came Rob's voice, part admonishing, part pleading, part questioning.

"Hey, Max! What the hell are you doing? Where are you going? They'll see you! You're gonna get yourself killed!"

"I'll take that chance," I shouted, showing mock bravado that I did not feel. "I don't think they can see us or hear us. We should find out for sure. Anyway, I think I know what this ceremony is all about."

As I walked toward the Altar Stone passing man after man, none of them showed the slightest reaction to my presence. About halfway into the center of the circle I stopped in front of one of the torchbearers. I stood inches from his face and waved my hand in front of his eyes. No reaction. I tried to touch his shoulder, but my hand went right through it. It was just as I had expected: an incomplete juncture of world lines.

I continued walking toward the Altar Stone. When I arrived there, I turned on my heels and looked out toward the Heel Stone. Again, just as I had suspected, the line of torches stretched out to the Heel Stone and beyond, an arrow pointing directly toward the northeast and to the glow in the sky. It was now clear why these men were there. The position of the stars and the moon had told us that this was late June. The direction of the sunrise was consistent with this assumption. In our time, it had been hypothesized that the position of the Heel Stone marked the rising of the midsummer sun. It was clear that these people were here for the purpose of orchestrating that very sunrise. We had just witnessed an event that before had only been hypothesized.

The only thing to do now was to wait for the event to unfold fully. Now convinced that it was safe, Rob followed me to the Altar Stone. We sat down, ignoring the priests that surrounded it, and gazed off toward the northeast. Over the next forth-five minutes, the glow got brighter and brighter, spilling luminous energy to all quarters of the sky. As the vista brightened, I noticed that the robed figures were fading. The brighter it got, the more difficult it was to see them. My attention was bifurcated, split between the ghost images of the people and the coming dawn.

When it looked as though the horizon would explode, the limb of the sun popped into view, slightly to the left of the Heel Stone. Over the next several minutes, it rose, as is its habit, along a diurnal circle, which at this latitude is tilted toward the south. As its altitude increased, so did its azimuth until, at an instant, the sun sat directly atop the Heel Stone, an inverted exclamation point to punctuate the event that was the raison d'être for the centuries of work that led to the construction of Stonehenge.

"Well, there it is," I said to Rob, motioning toward the sun. "There's the reason this place exists. It's amazing."

"Yeah, it's amazing all right, and it's also the answer to your question, the reason you came here," replied Rob.

"Whadaya mean?"

"I mean that what we witnessed here tonight was science. There was a prediction of the azimuth of the sunrise in the person of the Heel Stone. Then there was the observation of the sunrise to verify the prediction. Voila! End of story."

"No! What I saw wasn't science. Not the modern version."

"Why not?" asked Rob.

"Because science is more than a method. We all know the method. Formulate a question about nature. Generate an hypothesis that answers the question. From the hypothesis, make specific predictions. Finally, make observations to validate or refute the hypothesis. But science is also a philosophy. For example, both a geologist and a dowser seek to find water. One does it by using the scientific method of analyzing past data, and making observations, while the other uses . . . well, magic. They're both after the same end, but one, the geologist, is a scientist, the other is not. A scientist has the philosophy that there are rules of nature that must be obeyed and that these laws are knowable. There is no choice. There may be gods and goddesses, but those deities must obey those laws. The men we saw last night were bringing in the sunrise by propitiating the gods. That's what the ceremony was about. It meant that they perceived the gods as being in control. That's not science. That's a religion, a belief system. A belief expresses confidence in the truth or existence of something not susceptible to rigorous proof. But questions of science are susceptible to rigorous proof and, hence, are not the subject of a belief system.

"You can't have it both ways. Either the world is run by immutable law, or it's run by magic. In our time, the creationists, indeed all the fundamentalists in the world, would have you believe the world is run by magic, their wishful thinking, contrary to all objective observations. Such fuzzy thinking is dangerous because it yields self-serving results, such as 'there is no global warming' or 'old-growth forests are unimportant,' or 'I'm right, and if you disagree with me you're not only wrong, you're evil!'

"In the world today there are many examples of fuzzy thinking: astrology, religion, creationism, and myths such as the Bermuda Triangle, just to name a few. I used to think they were harmless, even sort of cute. I don't think so any more. These pseudo-scientific practices are the enemies of science in that they foster and maintain fuzzy thinking. The world is coming apart because of fuzzy thinking, and we can't suffer it any longer. Science may be cold and unfeeling, but that is the price of getting to the truth."

I looked at Rob and realized that he was no longer following my argument. His eyes had left mine and were sweeping the area. He had become distracted. "I'm sorry, I'm sorry," I said. "I'm running off at the mouth."

"No! It's not that," he said, letting out a long sigh of relief. "They're gone! When did they leave?"

"Or," I countered, "when did we cease to be able to see them?"

"You mean they might still be here?"

"Well," I said, "You know how difficult it is to see a projected image in the daylight. It might be the same with them."

"Are you saying that you think they were projected? It looked like they were."

"Well, if so," I responded, "it was like no projection I've ever seen. Think where the image was coming from. The light was actually coming from a point in space *between the stones and us*, not from the stones themselves as it would if they were acting as a projection screen. And remember the images before they crossed in front of the stones. There was nothing to project an image onto out there, yet the image was there nevertheless."

"So, what you are saying," said Rob, "is that these people are real."

"I know it seems impossible, but it goes along with everything else. It all seems impossible."

"Come on," said Rob, now looking at me incredulously. "Are you seriously saying that we've been projected into time and into the presence of transparent people that make no sounds?"

"Bear with me a moment," I said searching for words. "I'm not saying any of this is true or real. I'm just gathering observations and speculating. I know it's tempting to conclude that we're dreaming, and maybe we are. But think about it for a second. What makes a dream different from reality?"

"I don't know. Tell me," said Rob.

"Well I'm not sure either, but someone once told me that in a dream you don't get information from your five senses as much as you do when you're awake. The information of dreams is by and large cerebral. Weak on touch, smell, and taste. But my sense perceptions feel quite normal. All my senses tell me that this is reality!"

"So if you're right, we are approximately 2,500 years in the past, and the people who lived at that time are sort of here but not really. Is that what you're telling me?"

"I'm not telling you anything," I repeated. "It's just one hypothesis that fits the data."

"Well," said Rob, "I know a way we can disprove your hypothesis."

"How?" I said.

"In the best tradition of science, we can do an experiment. We can see if the guardhouse and the car are there. If they are, your hypothesis is SOL."

"That's a good idea," I said, feeling an anxious tug in my chest. I really didn't want to prove my hypothesis correct but, maybe, we were about to.

We walked to the base of the Trilithon where Rob's camera equipment was piled. We gathered the assorted boxes, sharing the load, and walked across the grass toward the spot where the path to the parking lot started. The morning was crisp, and the dew that had formed in the grass was working its way through my canvas tennis shoes, threatening to reach my socks. "My feet are getting wet," I remarked to Rob.

He looked at me quizzically for a moment before replying. "Poor baby," he said, with mock seriousness. We both broke out laughing, the foolish juxtaposition of my comment and the situation needing no elucidation.

"There's the path," said Rob, as he veered slightly to the left. In thirty seconds we were on it.

I started up the trail, anxious to get to the car that I hoped was there. But Rob had stopped walking. Slowly he put down the few boxes he was carrying and began looking around, sweeping the horizon in search of . . . something.

"What's the matter?" I asked.

"Is this the right path?" he countered.

"Sure it is," I said. "It's right where it's supposed to be and besides," I put my boxes down and turned to face the stones, now fifty yards distant, "this is the view we had when we first came down the path. It's burned into my memory for life. I have no doubt."

"OK," Rob replied. "I guess you're right, but . . ."

"But what?" I queried.

"Well," he said hesitantly, "I thought the path that we came down was paved. This one is dirt."

Before replying, I tried to reconstruct the events of the previous night. So much had happened since then. It felt as though a millennium had passed, and the irony was that maybe it had.

"I can't remember," I said, but deep down I thought he was right. I felt sure that the path had been paved last night. My optimism waned, and Rob seemed no better off.

"Well," I said, "I'm tired of being a spectator. First, we need to find out where we stand vis-à-vis the car. The car is our lifeline. Without it, trouble; with it, everything is OK."

While we talked, I bent down, scooped up Rob's equipment, and continued walking up the dirt path. The crest of the hill was thirty yards ahead. Just over the crest was the guardhouse, and beyond it, the car—at least if it were 1989. What we saw, or didn't see, when we crested the hill would make or break our whole day. We were now twenty yards from the crest, and we were both lost in our own private thoughts.

"Macheem, awake," Rob said suddenly.

I turned toward him. "What did you say?" I asked.

"Macheem, awake! We'll be late" The voice came from the distance, somewhere behind us. Although I heard it, I ignored it. The crest was only ten yards away now. I had to find out if the car was there. "Macheem, awake! I don't want to be late." The voice was more insistent.

"We need to know if the car is still there," I pleaded. "I'll come as soon as I find out."

"You'll come right now," said the voice, now coming from just a few feet over my head. "We cannot preside over the sunrise with our Chief Prescient still in his chambers. We've never missed an Insolation, and we're not going to start now."

"But I have to find the car," I moaned, struggling to open my eyes.

"What gibberish are you conjuring? What is a car?" said the voice, which I now recognized to be Robaan's.

"What is a car?" I repeated, confused.

"Mark this well, Macheem," said Robaan. "The Wain has already transited the upper meridian. The priesthood is fully assembled, and they have their offerings. The torch is lit, and the girl is prepared. The only thing we do not have is you. Neither Marduk nor your enemies will go lightly on us if we are late. Marduk will take the sunrise, and your enemies will take your head."

Still on my pad, I struggled into a sitting position, trying to clear my head. "What a strange vision I had while sleeping last night," I said to Robaan. "It was about visitors from the future who came to present-day Sarum and revealed their ideas to us—their strange, yet compelling, ideas."

"With your permission, Macheem, let us discuss your vision after the rising. The appointed hour grows near." Robaan was clearly worried.

"There will be no later," I said. "The vision fades even as I sit here."

"I'm sorry," said Robaan, "but we have no choice. Anyway, anything important you'll remember."

I was fully awake now, and the full weight of my responsibilities washed over me. The need to propitiate Marduk was my sacred trust. Without the proper ceremonies we were risking the cycles that made our lives possible. But something that one of the visitors said was gnawing at my subconscious. "There are rules that even He must obey," said the visitor. Could it be? Is it possible that Marduk is compelled to cause the sun to rise? And if He is compelled, He has no say. And if that is true, could it be that He has nothing to do with it whatsoever? How would we ever know if that were the case since we had been doing the ceremony for as long as memory served. But there was a way to test this idea.

"Robaan, have you ever wondered whether Marduk has any choice about the motion of the sun?"

"Marduk controls every aspect of the motion of all the heavenly bodies," Robaan recited, woodenly.

"Yes, I know what we were told by our teachers and what we tell our students. But how do we know that it's true? Can you remember a Prescient not bringing in the earliest sunrise? In fact have we ever had an unescorted sunrise or sunset at all?"

"Do not be foolish, Macheem. That's blasphemy!"

"Maybe so," I said, "but just the same, how do we know? I'll tell you how we'll know. We'll try it. Just this once. Tell the priests to leave the girl and the offerings here. In fact, we'll all stay here. We'll see if there's a difference. Then we'll know."

"Heresy!" said Robaan.

"No, not blasphemy and not heresy," I said. "Let's just call it"—I paused, searching for the right word and finding it materializing as from a dream, the first time the word had ever been used—*"an EXPERIMENT."*

Souls

She was not afraid. She knew the end was near, and she wanted it that way. She was confident that he would be waiting for her. For the last time, she closed her eyes. Her breathing became shallower and shallower. When the duty nurse entered her room to do her normal rounds, she found her patient dying. The nurse did nothing, for she knew her patient wanted it this way.

As she breathed out her final long breath, she saw the light. She was not surprised, for she had expected it. She had read enough stories about near-death experiences to know what would happen. She found that she had mobility. She was not walking or using her legs in any way. It was more like floating or flying. She knew the drill; she knew she had to get to the light. As a moth to the flame, she guided herself toward the luminescence. As she approached the brilliance, she saw no one waiting for her, but she was not disappointed or upset for she understood the reason. She realized, without surprise, that she understood everything. She didn't know how or why she understood everything, and she didn't care. She was without curiosity.

Her soul, for that's what it was, did not really enter the fourth plane unnoticed, for an Overseer from the eleventh level was on hand to witness the event. Instinctively the

Overseer knew her history: She (In reality, "she" no longer had a gender—no soul did.) had spent eighty-nine revolutions on the third level, all on a planet that its inhabitants call "Earth," in quadrant three of the mass accumulation called a "galaxy." It was her third time on level three (about average), and this time she had completed all of the requirements for passage to the next level.

There were eight billion souls on the third level—all on Earth. Many levels had only one receptacle for souls. Although this practice had been questioned in the past, there had never been a problem. According to the grand order, souls moved upward from level to level when they had learned the lessons that level had to offer—or they were returned to the level that they just left if they had not properly matured.

Up through the levels the souls rose, spending a lifetime at each one, a lifetime during which the universal lessons were learned. At the eleventh level, the level of the Overseers, these souls had progressed to the point where they understood enough of the workings of the first eleven levels that they could keep the celestial gears in motion. As such, the eleventh level housed the machinery of the multiverse.

But even those in the eleventh level, so well versed in "how" the levels worked, had no clue, not the slightest inkling, as to the "why" of the cosmos. To achieve that knowledge, a soul had to transit a near infinity of levels and an eternity of time. Only then, at level n (where n approaches infinity) are the now-enlightened souls privy to the truth of the cosmos, and once appraised, attain level n+1, where they merge with, indeed become, the cosmos itself, so that their energy powers the cosmos in the fulfillment of its appointed task—the reason for the whole thing.

And so the cosmos of levels goes, for an infinity of eternities, carrying out its vital task. Until one day . . . .

On Earth, the first real medical advances took place near the middle of the time period that they call their Twentieth Century. The advances were chemical in nature and strangely involved substances that selected for the most virile pathogens. Needless to say, this method failed. The second and greatest advance came about fifty revolutions later with the discovery of how to keep a patient's immune system from rejecting a foreign body; this so that a malfunctioning component could be replaced with a functioning component, either natural or artificial. All of these advances, however, did little to advance the longevity of the human animal.

The watershed moment in the history of the medical development of the life form called human came more than one hundred revolutions later with the development of the first working positronic brain, a complex device that, at the same time, solved the problems of capacity, longevity and versatility. Humans, in a moment of time, essentially became immortal. In the event of even the most catastrophic accident, the being could be totally reconstructed of artificial parts, right down to the brain, which was reprogrammed using the original as a template. The result was an artificial life form in which the soul was trapped, and was, for all practical purposes, immortal. The human technicians thought that they had done a good thing. Not everyone would agree.

One could argue that the Overseers should have been the first to notice it. That they didn't reflects more a seriousness of goal rather than an abdication of responsibility; all souls had as a primary responsibility the attainment of the next level. The functioning of the machinery and the order of things had never before been called into question.

No, the first to notice the situation was some underling prelate on level n-654. News of the unprecedented happening spread around the multiverse at the speed of thought. The ramifications of the "Earth-situation," as it was called, were discussed at the upper echelons of every level (except for levels one and two, where it was not understood, and level three, where, except for a small group of people who live on the northwest coast of a place called "California" and who call themselves "New Age," it was not believed).

But the truth could not be denied. These "humans," third level, no-account, slime-crawlers from a pip-squeak mote called "Earth," were threatening the entire mutiversal plan. Without a steady stream of souls from level three upward, in a very short time (multiversally speaking), the entire mechanism would come to a halt.

Since to do nothing was certain to bring the multiverse to the brink of chaos, the multiverse council, located, of course, in level n, decided to do whatever was necessary to start again the flow of souls to the upper levels. The solution decided upon was extreme. It was extreme because, since the beginning, all levels had subscribed to a prime doctrine of non-interference with other levels, for to interfere would potentially invalidate the grand experiment, which, after all, was the purpose of the whole thing. So, rather than redesign and reinitiate, the council took action.

They had been floating in the ice-cold vacuum of space for about four billion earthly revolutions. They were, as yet, nowhere near one another, but they were, nevertheless, of a kind: two high-density balls of neutron material (the humans called them "neutron stars"), stabilized against the crushing force of gravity by the mutual repulsion of the component neutrons.

It didn't take much of a push—just enough to impart a ΔV of .0000067 mi./sec to one of the neutron cores. But when it was carried out by a representative of the level n council, it was enough to put the two masses on a collision path, with the point of impact a mere 0.43 light years from Earth.

No one witnessed the impact. One moment there were two stars speeding on their respective courses. In the next second, there was a blinding flash as the two masses merged creating a single object (a "black hole" to the inhabitants of Earth) with enough gravity to overcome all other forces in the multiverse. The ensuing catastrophic collapse compressed the outer envelope of the body to fusion temperatures. In the next instant, thermonuclear reactions created all of the heavy elements in the multiverse and, as a by-product, gamma rays—lots of gamma rays.

These gamma rays, traveling at the speed of light, spread out into space and reached Earth in less than half a year. In an instant, the half of the planet facing the source of radiation was sterilized. But since the blast of gamma rays was two light hours thick, the sterilization continued as the planet rotated more life forms into the path of the beam. When it was over, three quarters of the life on Earth was extinguished, catapulting billions of souls into the void.

In an instant, the civilization of humans was no more and disappearing with it, their brief foray into immortality. The cycling of souls resumed and the grand experiment was saved. The Multiversal Council nodded in approval when informed of the successful intervention and went on to the next order of business.

Made in the USA
Lexington, KY
02 December 2011